"You see, woman y and I stil you did..."

"Can't you?" he murmured huskily. "Aside from my wealth, I had nothing to offer you, but you appeared to want very little." Duarte studied her with spectacular dark eyes that had the most scorching effect on her heated flesh. "Apart from *me*... and you wanted me like you wanted air to breathe. That was then. This is now and much has changed." Duarte surveyed her with satisfaction. "But not, I think, your hunger for me."

"Well, that's where you're dead wrong...."

Duarte reached for her, and before she had the chance to blink, his hard sensual mouth came down on hers with all the explosive force and expertise of a heat-seeking missile. Her whole body seemed to surge up and into his, instantly fired by the burning head of desire he could unleash.

"Duarte..." she gasped feverishly. "Duarte—"

"Our son is crying. You should go to him."

Lynne Graham

DUARTE'S CHILD

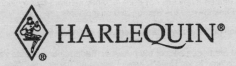

HARLEQUIN®

TORONTO • NEW YORK • LONDON
AMSTERDAM • PARIS • SYDNEY • HAMBURG
STOCKHOLM • ATHENS • TOKYO • MILAN • MADRID
PRAGUE • WARSAW • BUDAPEST • AUCKLAND

ISBN 0-373-12199-7

DUARTE'S CHILD

First North American Publication 2001.

Copyright © 2001 by Lynne Graham.

CHAPTER ONE

'WHAT action do you want me to take?' the private investigator enquired.

Duarte Avila de Monteiro let the silence linger and continued to gaze out at his stunning view of the City of London. *She'd been found.* Sudden success after so many fruitless months of searching felt intoxicating. He would retrieve his son. Her too, of course. She was still his wife. He refused to think of her by name. He refused to personalise her in any way.

'Do nothing,' Duarte responded without expression.

His wealthy client was a total emotion-free zone, the investigator decided in fascination. He'd just given the guy the news that he had finally traced his runaway wife and the infant son he had still to meet—and yet nothing was to be done?

'Leave the file on my desk,' Duarte continued in a tone of dismissal. 'There will be a substantial bonus when you present the bill for your services.'

On his way past what he assumed to be the secretary's desk in the ante-room outside, the investigator paused: the secretary was the most stunning Nordic blonde he had ever laid eyes on. 'Your boss is kind of chilling,' he murmured confidentially.

'My boss is a brilliant financial genius and also my lover,' the blonde whispered in a voice as cutting as slashing glass meeting tender skin. 'You just lost your bonus.'

Rearing back in startled disbelief at that poisonous response, the young investigator stared at the beautiful blonde, aghast.

5

'Shall I call Security to have you removed?' she added sweetly.

Within his imposing office, Duarte was pouring himself a brandy and contemplating the immediate future. He had an overwhelming desire to muster his entire security team and spring a middle-of-the-night assault on his estranged wife and child's accommodation. He *had* to move fast before she disappeared again with his son. His mobile phone gripped between lean brown fingers, he tensed and then frowned. For an instant, he could not believe that he had even contemplated such an act of madness. He could wait until morning... Well, he could wait until dawn at least.

He stabbed out the number for the head of his protection team. 'Mateus? You will proceed to the address I am about to give you. There you will find a caravan—'

'A *caravan*...?'

'Which contains my wife and my child,' Duarte admitted with a grimace at the sheer incredulity he could hear in Mateus's voice. 'You will ensure that if that caravan moves so much as an inch it will be followed. You will also be discreet while treating this as a matter of the utmost urgency and importance.'

'We'll leave immediately, sir,' Mateus confirmed, sounding shaken. 'Your faith in us won't be misplaced.'

'Discretion, Mateus.'

Duarte made a second call to put his private jet on standby for the next day. Was he planning to kidnap them both? She was his wife. Kidnapping was a crime. *She* had kidnapped his son. *Inferno!* A bloody caravan! Duarte gritted his even white teeth, a flash of white-hot rage threatening his hard self-discipline. She was bringing *his* son up in a caravan while she mucked around with horses. Who was looking after their child while she devoted her attention to four-legged animals?

Emily—safe, quiet, humble and as easily read as an open

book—a young woman unlikely to rock any boats. How had he *ever* thought that? With a raw-edged laugh, Duarte drained the brandy. He had picked her quite deliberately for those unassuming qualities. He'd given her everything that would have kept most women purring with delighted contentment. Fabulous wealth, a selection of luxurious homes and glittering social occasions at which she could show off her equally fabulous jewellery. His reward for his unquestioning generosity? She'd betrayed her marriage vows and his trust: she'd got into bed with another man. Obviously quiet women needed to be *watched*.

One of his medieval ancestors had murdered his unfaithful wife and got off scot-free because it had been regarded as an act of cleansing the family honour, rather than a crime. Duarte could not contemplate ever laying rough hands on any woman, even his estranged wife, no matter how enraged he was by her shameless behaviour. Then, Duarte never lost control in any field. He would deal with the situation as he saw fit. Walling her up alive would not have given him the slightest satisfaction and he could only assume his ancestor had been a seriously sick pervert.

There were other infinitely more subtle ways of controlling women. And Duarte knew *all* the ways. Duarte had never practised those arts on his seemingly innocent and shy little wife. So she was in for a surprise or two in the near future...

'I just don't understand why you have to move on,' Alice Barker confessed. 'I can drum up enough eager learners to keep you employed right through the year.'

Stiff with tension, Emily evaded the older woman's questioning gaze. Small in stature and slight of build, she wore her long curly red hair in a sensible plait. 'I don't usually stay anywhere for long—'

'You have a six-month-old baby. It's not so easy to stay

on the move with a young child,' Alice pointed out. 'I need a permanent riding instructor and the job's yours if you want it. My stables would profit from you staying on just as much as you would—'

Feeling the dialogue had gone far enough when there was not the smallest chance of her changing her mind about leaving, Emily lifted her bright head. Her aquamarine eyes were troubled and embarrassed, for she hated to turn down an offer that she would have loved to accept. However, telling the truth about why she had to refuse wasn't an option. 'I'm sorry, but we really do have to leave—'

'Why?' The older woman's weathered face was set in stubborn lines.

Emily's fair complexion was flushed with discomfiture. 'I guess I'm a rolling stone—'

'I don't believe that. I know travelling folk and you don't have that restlessness. You could have a comfortable home and job here with friends—'

'You're making this very difficult for me, Alice—'

The older woman tilted back her greying head and studied Emily with wry eyes. 'Maybe I'm hoping that you'll come clean and admit that you're running from something or somebody...and that the *only* thing keeping you on the road is fear of that somebody or something catching up with you!'

Emily turned very pale at that disturbingly accurate assessment.

'Of course, I suspected that you might be in some sort of fix,' Alice Barker admitted with a sympathetic look. 'You're too reserved and, by nature, I'd say you were a much more relaxed person. You're also too nervous of strangers.'

'I haven't broken the law or anything,' Emily responded in a strained undertone. 'But I'm afraid that's as much as I can say.'

But even as she made that assurance, she wondered if it was *still* true. Had she broken any English law in what she had done? How was she to know when she had not taken legal advice? She'd been on the run for eight months and she'd not got back in touch with her family or indeed anyone else during that period.

'Are you trying to shake off an abusive boyfriend?' Alice was keen to get to the root of Emily's problems. 'Why don't you let me help you? Running away never solves anything.'

Dismayed by her companion's persistence, Emily muttered in a rush, 'You've been really great to us. I'll never forget that but we *have* to leave first thing tomorrow.'

Recognising the sheen of tears in Emily's eyes, Alice sighed and gave the younger woman an awkward hug. 'If you change your mind, there'll always be a bed here for you.'

Closing the caravan door behind her, Alice trudged back down the lane to the stable block to lock up for the evening. Emily drew in a slow, deep, shaken breath. One thing that Alice had said had hit Emily on a very tender nerve. *Running away never solves anything*. That was so horribly true, Emily conceded heavily. Nothing had been solved or settled. It was eight months since she had left Portugal. She had run home to her family for support but her family had treated her like an escaped convict.

'Don't think that we're going to get involved!' Emily's mother had pronounced in furious dismissal. 'So please don't embarrass us with the details of your marital problems.'

'Go home to your husband. You're not staying here with us,' her father had told her in outrage.

'Have you gone out of your tiny mind?' Her eldest sister, Hermione, had demanded. 'What do you think your walking out on your marriage is likely to do to the family business? If Duarte blames us, we'll *all* be ruined!'

'You really are an absolute idiot to come here,' her other sister, Corinne, had said with stinging scorn. 'None of us are going to help you. Did you really expect us to react any other way?'

The answer to that frank question would have been yes but Emily had been too devastated by that mass rejection to respond. *Yes*, time and time again through childhood and adolescence and indeed right up to the age of twenty when she married, Emily had fondly hoped to receive some small sign that her family loved her. That blind faith had sunk without trace for the last time. She'd finally accepted that she was the cuckoo in the family nest, an outsider who was both resented and unwelcome and that nothing was *ever* likely to change that reality.

Why it should be that way she'd never understood. Yet she was painfully aware that had she got the chance to sit down and tell the honest truth about why her marriage had fallen apart, she would undoubtedly have been shown the door by her family even more quickly.

She'd had to face the fact that, whatever she chose to do, she was on her own. So she'd sold her engagement ring. With the proceeds, she'd bought an old car and a caravan and she had hit the road to make a living the only way she could. Travelling around the countryside from one stables to another, she offered her services for a few weeks as a riding instructor and then moved on to pastures new. The longer she stayed in one place, the greater the chance that she would be tracked down.

Of course, Duarte was looking for both her and his child. Duarte Avila de Monteiro, the terrifyingly powerful and even more terrifyingly wealthy banker she had foolishly married. His brilliance in the world of finance was a living legend.

When Duarte had asked Emily to marry him, she had been stunned for she hadn't been beautiful, sophisticated or even rich. Furthermore, her relatives might like to give themselves airs and graces in polite company but, though her family could not bear to have it mentioned, Emily's grandfather had been a milkman. So, understandably, Emily had been overwhelmed that Duarte Avila de Monteiro should decide to marry her humble and ordinary self. That he didn't love her…well, so nothing was perfect, she had told herself. At the outset, she'd been full of cheerful and trusting hopes for the future. Adoring him like a silly schoolgirl, she'd simply marvelled at her own good luck.

Although she had been in awe of her husband, she had never feared him, not the way others did. People were afraid to cross his reserve and offend him. People were afraid of his unapologetic ruthlessness. She'd been stupid *not* to fear him, Emily conceded heavily with the knowledge of hindsight. A wretched light in her troubled eyes, she reached into her son Jamie's cot and lifted his warm, solid little body up into her arms. Eight months ago, Duarte had threatened to take her baby from her as soon as he was born and raise him without her. Within days of being told of that appalling threat, Emily had fled Portugal in a panic.

But unhappily there was no escape from the reality that she had destroyed her own marriage. She had been the guilty partner. It was *her* fault that Duarte had demanded a separation, *her* fault that Duarte had ultimately decided that she ought to be deprived of their child as well. Indeed, in recent months, Emily had started feeling even worse over the fact that Duarte was being deprived of the right to even *see* his own son. Only her terror of losing custody of Jamie and her fearful awareness that she had neither Duarte's money nor influence had triumphed over her guilty conscience.

Now, however, Emily was finally facing the immaturity

of her own behaviour. It was time that she went to see a lawyer and found out exactly where she stood. It was time she *stopped* running...

Yet how did she deal with Duarte? And how would Duarte now deal with her? In spite of herself, she shivered as discouraging memories engulfed her. During their separation, Duarte had exiled her to the country house in the Douro for the winter. She had lived there alone for three months, hoping against hope that he would eventually agree to see her and talk to her again and that the great divide between them might somehow be miraculously mended. But that had been such a naive dream.

For Duarte, Emily thought painfully, would be happy to acquire a son and dispense with the baby machine who had produced that son. For really that was all she had ever been to her gorgeous husband...a baby machine. For what other reason had he married her? Certainly not for love, lust or loneliness. Childlessness was a disaster to the average Portuguese male and Duarte had an illustrious name. The Monteiro family could trace their aristocratic lineage back to the thirteenth century and, naturally, Duarte had wanted a child to carry on into the next generation.

Accustomed to early rising, Emily was up before dawn the following morning.

She'd packed the night before. After feeding Jamie and making herself some toast and tea, she collapsed his cot and stowed it safely away. Living in a small caravan had taught her to be tidy. As she slid into a pair of old navy jodhpurs and pulled on a voluminous grey sweater to combat the early morning chill, she watched her son. Sitting on the carpet in the compact seating area, Jamie was chewing industriously on the corner of a horse magazine.

Emily darted over and detached the magazine from his mouth. 'No, Jamie...here's your ring.'

Presented with the teething ring which had been chilled specially for his use, Jamie dropped it again and his bottom lip came out, brown eyes filming over with tears as he tried without success to reach for the magazine again. Sweeping her son up into her arms, Emily cuddled him and wondered why he loathed the teething ring which would have been so much kinder to his sore gums.

As always the warm baby smell of Jamie sent a great wave of love through her and she hugged him tight. He had Duarte's black hair and golden skin and the same shape eyes as her. Right now, because he had another new tooth on the way, he had pink flushed cheeks and he looked absolutely adorable in his red sweatshirt top and tiny jeans.

Checking that she had secured everything moveable, Emily decided to put Jamie out in his car seat. She had said her goodbyes the night before and all she still had to do was hitch up the caravan to the car.

It was a fresh spring day and the breeze blew back the Titian red curls from her brow. With Jamie balanced on her hip, she unlocked the passenger door of the car. Strapping her son into his seat and stowing the baby bag of supplies that went everywhere with them, she chatted with greater cheer than she felt to him. 'I timed this so that we would see the six o'clock train passing at the crossing. Choo-choo, Jamie—'

'Choo...' he seemed to sound out but she was prepared to concede that it might have been the wishful thinking of a proud mother.

Another day, another place, Emily reflected wearily and it was no longer the smallest thrill to contemplate the unknown that lay ahead. She had stayed longer than was wise at Alice Barker's stables, not only because she liked the older woman but also because she had been in dire need of a period of regular employment and earnings. Running even an old car was expensive; she had recently had to renew her insurance and replace the whole exhaust system. So, once again, she had little cash in reserve.

As she stuck her car keys in the ignition and turned, intending to hitch up the caravan, she heard an angry shout and then another. It sounded like Alice. Frowning in dismay, Emily hurried past the caravan to see what was happening. At the rear entrance to the stables, she saw a sight that shook her. Alice Barker was standing with a shotgun trained on a man.

'Just you tell me right now what you were doing!' Alice was demanding furiously.

As Emily rushed automatically to support the older woman, she heard the man speak and she caught several words. Alice's trespasser was striving to apologise in Portuguese. Emily froze in her tracks. *Portuguese?*

'I caught this chappie trying to creep up on your caravan!' Alice called to Emily with patent disgust. 'One of the peeping Toms, one of those filthy perverts…that's what I've caught. Just as well he doesn't seem to speak a word of English. I shouldn't think he's saying anything any decent woman would want to hear! Reach into my pocket and get my phone, and we'll ring the police!'

But Emily did not move an inch. Every scrap of colour draining from her slanting cheekbones, she stared at the stocky, well-built Portuguese male in his smart city suit. It was Mateus Santos, Duarte's security chief. Her tummy churned, her brain refusing to move at speed. The older man was as white as his own shirtfront, evidently not having expected to be greeted by a very angry woman with a shotgun when he came snooping.

'Emily!' Alice barked impatiently.

Mateus's strained gaze swerved to Emily's stilled figure with perceptible relief. *'Doña Emilia…'* he greeted her and followed that up with a hasty flood of Portuguese.

Emily understood a little more of the language than she

could actually speak and she caught the gist of his appeal. Mateus was asking her to tell Alice that he was no danger to anybody. Only that wasn't quite true, Emily decided in sudden total panic. If Mateus was at the stables, it meant that Duarte had tracked *her* down and that Duarte now knew where she was. 'I know this man, Alice. He's no threat, but please keep him here until I can get away—'

'Emily...what on earth is going on?' Alice demanded in bewilderment.

But Emily was already speeding back towards her car. Where Mateus was, Duarte would soon follow. She jumped into the driver's seat and then realised that she had still to hitch up the caravan.

With a gasp of frustration, she began to reverse the car and then dashed out again to haul at the caravan with frantic hands. The task accomplished, she was in the act of swinging back into her car when she saw the bonnet of a big silver vehicle filter into the mouth of the lane she needed to go down to make her exit.

Heart thumping somewhere in the region of her convulsing throat, Emily stared in absolute horror at the limousine. Duarte! It could only be Duarte behind those tinted windows. Just as suddenly, she unfroze again and flung herself into her own car. The ground siding the lane was unfenced and reasonably level. She could drive *around* the limo! Firing the engine, she slammed the door. Within six feet of the long luxury vehicle seeking to block her escape, she turned the steering wheel and took her car off the lane on to the rough grass verge. The caravan bounced in protest and the vibrations shook the car but, within the space of thirty seconds, she was back on the concrete lane again, the caravan still in tow.

She would go to a lawyer, Emily told herself frantically. She would stop at the first legal firm she saw and beg for an appointment and advice. She was not going to risk facing Duarte alone in case he simply took Jamie from her and flew him out to Portugal. Hadn't she read horror stories about disaffected foreign husbands taking that kind of action when their marriages to their British wives broke down?

And, worst of all, wouldn't Duarte have grounds to argue that *she* had virtually pulled the *same* stunt on him? Jamie was six months old and his own father had yet to meet him. What right did she have to keep them apart? An agony of conflict and guilt in her gaze as she questioned what she was doing, Emily pulled out of the lane on to the twisting country road that lay beyond.

Duarte would attempt to follow her but she was at an advantage for she knew the area. How could she take the chance of trusting Duarte when he might take Jamie away from her? She would be lucky to ever see her child again. Where she was concerned, her estranged husband would not be feeling the slightest bit sympathetic or reasonable. Why, oh why, oh why had she waited this long before acknowledging that it was past time she sorted out the whole mess?

Rounding a corner on the road, Emily had to start immediately slackening speed. A shaken laugh shorn of any humour was torn from her tight throat. The railway crossing lay ahead. The warning lights were flashing and the automatic barriers were coming down signifying that a train was about to pass through. She was trapped for a good five minutes by the very train she had promised Jamie he would see as a treat. By the time the express finally thundered past the barriers, Emily was studying her driving mirror and watching the silver limo appear behind her on the road. Caught! Fate had not been on her side. In a gesture of frustrated defeat, Emily lifted one of her hands from the steering wheel and struck it down on the dash board.

She felt a prick like a sharp stinging needle in the side

of her hand. Blinking, she glanced down and gaped in dawning horror at the big bee crawling away. It wasn't the season, a little voice screamed inside her, it wasn't the season yet for bees! She hadn't replaced her allergy kit when she had mislaid it over the winter. She dropped her hand down to open the driver's door. Already she felt like she was moving in slow motion; already she could feel the sensation of her heartbeat starting to race.

She lurched out of the car. She struggled to focus on the formidably tall and dark male striding towards her but she raised her hands to her face instead, feeling the tenderness and the heat there, knowing that her skin had probably begun to swell and redden. 'Sting...bee!' she framed jerkily.

'Where's your adrenaline kit?' Duarte demanded, instantly grasping the crisis and reacting at speed.

With enormous effort she blinked and connected momentarily with stunning dark golden eyes that she would never have dared to meet had she been in full control of herself. 'Lost...'

'*Meu Deus!* The nearest doctor?' Duarte caught hold of her as she doubled over with the pain piercing her abdomen and vented a startled gasp. 'Emily...a hospital...a doctor?' he raked down at her with raw urgency. '*Where?*'

It was such an effort for her to concentrate, to speak. 'Village through the crossing,' she wheezed.

She was conscious of movement as he carried her, the roar of car engines and raised voices in Portuguese but she was in too much pain to try to see what was happening. She opened her swollen eyes with a grimace of discomfort, for her whole body was hurting. She registered that she was lying in Duarte's arms inside an unfamiliar car and was suddenly terrified that everyone had forgotten about her baby. 'Jamie...?'

'*He* will be OK...'

Even in the state she was in, the sense that she was now

hearing his voice from the end of a long dark tunnel, she picked up on that stress. *She* might not be OK. She had been fifteen years old when it was impressed on her after an adverse reaction to a bee sting that she must go nowhere without her adrenaline kit. She had been too scared not to be sensible but, as the years passed without further incident, she had gradually become rather more careless. 'If I die…' she slurred with immense difficulty because the inside of her mouth and her tongue were swollen, 'You get Jamie…only fair—'

'*Por amar de Deus*, you are *not* going to die, Emily,' Duarte cut in savagely, lifting up her head, rearranging her with careful hands because she was starting to struggle for breath. 'I will not allow it.'

But before she lost consciousness, all she could think about was that it *would* be only fair if Duarte got Jamie. It was a punishment for her to be near Duarte again. It made it impossible for her to evade her own tormenting memories. Eleven months ago, one instant of hesitation had cost Emily her marriage—Duarte had found her in the arms of another man.

She'd let Toby kiss her and she still couldn't explain why, even to herself. At the time she had been desperately unhappy and Toby had astonished her when he had told her that he loved her. In her whole life, nobody had *ever* told Emily that they loved her and she had never expected to hear those words. Certainly, she'd given up hope of ever inspiring such high-flown feelings in her gorgeous but essentially indifferent husband.

While she'd been frantically wondering what she could say that would not hurt Toby's feelings, Toby had grabbed her and kissed her. Why hadn't she pushed him away? She'd not been attracted to Toby, nor had she wanted that bruising kiss. Yet she'd still stood there and *allowed* him to kiss her. She'd been unfaithful to her husband and there was no justifying that betrayal of trust to a male as proud and uncompromising as Duarte. In the aftermath, she'd been so distraught with shame that she had made a total hash of convincing her husband that that single kiss had been the *only* intimacy she had ever shared with Toby. Convinced that she'd been having an affair, Duarte had demanded a separation, even though she was four months pregnant with their child.

Emily's eyes opened and she snatched in a great whoosh of oxygen to fill her starved lungs.

The injection of adrenaline brought about an almost instantaneous recovery but she was severely disorientated and she didn't know where she was. As she began to sit up, scanning the unfamiliar faces surrounding her and recognising a nurse in her uniform, she gasped, 'What...*where*?'

'You just had a very narrow escape. You were in anaphylactic shock.' The older man gave her a relieved smile. 'You're in the cottage hospital. I'm the duty doctor. We administered the adrenaline jab in the nick of time.'

'Take it easy and lie down for a minute,' the nurse advised. 'Do you feel sick?'

As Emily rested back again, she moved her swimming head in a negative motion. After that initial buzzing return of energy which had revitalised her, she now felt weak as a kitten. She was on a trolley, not a bed, and as the cluster of medical staff surrounding her parted because the emergency was over she saw Duarte looming just feet away. She raised trembling hands to her still tender face, felt the swelling that was still there and knew that she had to look an absolute fright. In addition, the very minute that foolish thought occurred to her, she became aware of her own demeaning vulnerability.

For a split second, it was like time stood still. Her dazed aquamarine eyes wide above her spread fingertips connected with his spectacular dark golden gaze. His eyes were rich as the finest of vintage wine but utterly without expression. She could feel her heartbeat quicken, the wretched inescapable burst of liquid heat surge between her slender thighs. He came, he saw, he conquered, she misquoted, shaken to her depths by her own helpless response. From the first moment it had been like that with Duarte.

There had been a wild uncontrollable longing that had nothing to do with sense or caution. Something that had come so naturally to her, something that had been rooted so deep in her psyche that only death could have ended her addiction to him. He'd drawn her like a magnet and, what was more, he had known it from the first instant of their eyes meeting.

But their marriage had been a disaster for both of them, she reminded herself miserably. The more she'd loved him, the more she had become agonised by his inherent indifference. Impervious to her every attempt to breach that barrier, he had broken her heart. She had even been hurt by his satisfaction when she fell pregnant, for it was a satisfaction he had never shown in her alone. The old sick shame filled her as she recalled that fatal kiss which had cost her everything that mattered to her. She had finally broken through Duarte's reserve only to discover that *all* she could touch was his pride and his honour.

'I could strangle you for your carelessness, Emily...' Duarte breathed in a curiously ragged undertone.

'What *you* need is a good cup of tea. You've had a nasty shock too,' the middle-aged nurse informed Duarte in a brisk and cheerful interruption. Unaccustomed to being addressed as if he was a large child, he looked sincerely startled.

A porter began to wheel out the trolley on which Emily lay. As the nurse had spoken, Emily had finally recognised the ashen quality of Duarte's usually vibrant skin tone and the sheen of perspiration on his sculpted dark features. She closed her eyes, acknowledging the truth of the older woman's assurance. She had almost died on him. Evidently, he was relieved that she had survived. Maybe he did not hate her *quite* as much as she had assumed he did.

But then hatred meant a strong emotion where the target was concerned, didn't it? And Duarte had never felt *any* particularly strong emotion in her direction. A pain that felt almost physical enclosed her and she shut her eyes in self-defence. She knew that she had never had the power to hide her feelings from him and she had not the courage to meet his eyes levelly.

'Your husband has had the fright of his life,' the kindly nurse soothed her in a small empty side ward. 'When your child runs out in front of a car, you shout at him afterwards because you're angry and afraid that you almost lost him.'

'Yes…' Emily was rolled gently into a bed. She did not like to say that Duarte's most likely feeling now was one of complete exasperation and contempt. In her position, he would never have made the mistake of being without that life-saving adrenaline kit.

'Why am I being put to bed?' Emily asked, finding herself being deftly undressed.

'The doctor wants us to keep you under observation for a few hours just to be sure that you have no adverse reactions.'

Helped into a hospital nightdress in a faded print and left alone, Emily lay back against the pillows, anxiously wondering who exactly had charge of Jamie and how her baby was coping with her sudden disappearance. Almost at the same moment as she was thinking that the nurse reappeared, cradling Jamie, who was howling at the top of his lungs. 'I believe this little soul is yours and he wants his mum!'

Emily opened her arms and Jamie grabbed on to her the

instant he was brought within her reach. 'Who was looking after him?'

'The older man, who arrived just after your husband brought you in. He doesn't speak any English. He was out at Reception trying to calm your little boy down.'

Mateus Santos, she assumed, a committed bachelor who was probably pretty useless with young children. Jamie snuffled into weary silence against her shoulder just as Duarte appeared in the open doorway. He stilled when he saw the child in her arms and the nurse slipped out, leaving them alone.

Her tummy twisting, her eyes veiled, Emily muttered awkwardly, 'Have you seen Jamie yet?'

'No...Mateus brought him here in your car. My time was taken up tending to you,' Duarte admitted curtly.

Jamie had a death grip on her. He was going through that stage of disliking strangers that many babies went through around his age. He resisted being turned round and pushed his dark head under her chin. He'd had quite enough of excitement and strangers for one morning. It was anything but the best moment for Duarte to meet his son for the first time.

'Duarte...I'm *so* sorry!' Emily heard herself admit with her usual impulsiveness, a sob catching in her aching throat. 'I am so very sorry for everything...'

'That cuts no ice with me,' Duarte responded with eyes that were as hard and bright as burnished steel, cold derision etched in every line of his starkly handsome features as he studied her shaken face. 'How dare you drag my son round the countryside in a caravan like a gipsy? How dare you put me in the position where I have to answer to the police merely because I attempted to *see* my own child? And how dare you look at me now and insult my intelligence with that pathetic excuse of a word, "sorry"?'

CHAPTER TWO

'THE... police?' Emily stammered even more aghast.

'Since I married you, you have brought me only shame and dishonour.' Duarte breathed starkly, his controlled lack of volume far more dramatic than any shout.

'The police?' Emily whispered again shakily, her sensitive tummy tying itself into sick knots.

'Your employer, Mrs Barker, reported your great escape from her property *and* my natural pursuit. She expressed concern for your safety. Two police officers are now waiting outside for my explanation.' Duarte drew himself up to his full imposing six-foot-four-inch height and squared his broad shoulders with all the fierce pride of his ancestors in his bearing, but sheer outrage glittered in his condemning gaze.

'Duarte—'

'If you dare to lie and suggest that I have abused you or mistreated you in *any* way whatsoever, I will fight you for custody of my son! Is that quite clear?'

As crystal. Chilled to the temperature of ice by that announcement, Emily trembled. Her arms wrapped more tightly still round Jamie. Impervious to that old chestnut that children were always disturbed by maternal tension, Jamie had dropped off to sleep against her shoulder. With that single threat, Duarte had deprived Emily of voice, breath and hope that their differences could be resolved. She was in shock and could not have said why. After all, if Duarte had been prepared to separate her from her child the instant he was born, he could only be even keener to do so after the months that had since passed.

But then, eight months ago, Duarte's words of threat had *not* been spoken to her face. It was only thanks to her friend, Bliss that Emily had learned of Duarte's plans. Bliss had overheard Duarte state his punitive intentions to his lawyer and had forewarned Emily of her estranged husband's intentions.

Now quite unable to dislodge her arrested attention from Duarte, she scanned his fabulous bone structure for some sign of softening and found none. He meant what he was saying. Standing there straight and tall and unashamed and more beautiful than any male had the right to be. Like a dark angel. Even emanating aggressive vibrations, he was absolutely gorgeous, possessed of the kind of sleek, dark, bronzed good looks that turned female heads wherever he went. Why the heck hadn't she smelled a rat the size of the Titanic when he proposed marriage to someone as ordinary as she was? And why on earth had he neglected to mention his tragic first marriage? For any heart that Duarte ever had was buried in the grave with his childhood sweetheart.

'Is that understood, Emily?' Duarte prompted lethally.

Dully she nodded, dredging her attention from him in shrinking apprehension. To think that on several occasions recently she had anxiously wondered if she had misjudged him! No, there was no room to suspect *now* that Bliss might have misunderstood what she'd overheard or that Emily herself had overreacted to something said in anger and never ever intended to be acted upon. After the way she'd behaved, Duarte did not believe she *deserved* to have their child.

'Yes...' Emily turned her pinched face away and rested her cheek against Jamie's soft, sweet-smelling baby skin to comfort herself. Every which way she looked, she had done wrong, and there was no point offending even more by seeking to defend herself.

'I have no wish to part you from our son,' Duarte stated in a grim undertone. 'He needs you very much.'

'Do you really think that?' she whispered shakily.

'I say nothing that I don't mean. Give me Jamie now that he is asleep,' Duarte urged moving forward. 'Mrs Barker followed my security team here. She has offered to take care of our son until you are released from hospital. I understand she is familiar to him.'

Taut with suspicion, Emily held fast to Jamie's precious weight, but then she saw Alice appearing in the doorway with a look of discomfiture on her face. The older woman was carrying Jamie's baby bag. 'I'll look after Jamie, Emily. It's the least that I can do.'

'I will leave you both and deal with the police,' Duarte delivered coolly.

Alice grimaced and sank down at the foot of the bed. 'How was I to know he was your husband? I thought Mafia hitmen were descending on us and I was really frantic when they took off after you!'

'You didn't know what was happening…and I was totally stupid,' Emily groaned in remorse. 'I made things even worse by trying to run again. I just panicked and then I got stung—'

'And your husband, whom I thought was a dead ringer for the Godfather at his most glamorous, *saved* your life.' Alice winced. 'I feel so awful now for calling in the police and now they *won't* go away until everyone's explained themselves about twenty times over.'

'It's OK… It's all my fault. I always do the wrong thing,' Emily mumbled heavily. 'Particularly around Duarte—'

'Not much of a husband if he makes you feel like that. Maybe, to make me feel a little more relaxed about all this, you could tell me that he is really wonderful.'

'He *is*… I was the one who wrecked everything.' Emily sighed.

By wanting more than Duarte had ever offered, she'd made herself unhappy. She'd had a hunger to be loved and, if not loved, at least needed. But Duarte had not needed her either. She had just felt like another one of his many possessions with no true existence or purpose without him. She had never had much confidence but, flung in at the deep end of a world so very different from her own, she had sunk like a stone, becoming even more shy and awkward. By the time of their separation, she'd gone from having low self-esteem to having no self-esteem at all.

Alice left with Jamie. Then a very weary-looking police sergeant made a brief visit to Emily's bedside to confirm that she had no complaint to make against her husband. Having made that assurance while cringing at the thought of what Duarte must have undergone, Emily fell asleep and did not awaken until lunch arrived on a noisy trolley. The doctor called in to have a brief word with her and tell her that she was free to leave. As she had no appetite for food, she slid straight out of bed. Removing her clothes from the cabinet, she got dressed again.

Mateus Santos was waiting at Reception to escort her out to the limousine.

Duarte was seated in the back of the limo. Emily climbed in and sat down at the furthest point from Duarte that she could contrive. 'What now?' she asked tightly.

'We'll pick up Jamie and then we're going home.'

The silence lay between them, deep as a swamp and twice as treacherous.

Emily swallowed hard. *Going home?* She had not yet given him a direct look. Now she turned her head, her throat tight, her sea-green eyes strained. 'Just like that?'

'Just like that,' Duarte confirmed, skimming her a veiled glance from his dark, deep-set eyes. 'I had your possessions cleared from the car and the caravan and packed. I also told Mateus to dispose of both vehicles as you will have no further use for them.'

That was the moment that Emily appreciated that she now possessed only the clothes she stood up in. Her fingers closed over the ragged cuffs of her old sweater in an effort to contain an almost overwhelming sense of being trapped. 'It would have been nice if you had asked me what I wanted to do with them.'

'But then, all that concerned me was what I wanted,' Duarte murmured with velvet soft cool, reaching forward to sweep up the car phone as it buzzed.

Going home? He was taking them straight back to Portugal. From below her lashes, she studied him, nervous as a cat on hot bricks. The hard smooth line of his high cheekbones in profile, the classic perfection of his arrogant nose, the tough angular jawline slightly blue-shadowed by the hint of returning stubble. He was incredibly good-looking and sexy and she found it very difficult to resist the urge to stare when his attention was distracted from her. She listened to him talk in Portuguese, as smooth and cool as if he had not just dramatically reclaimed his runaway wife and child. No, indeed, it might have been any ordinary day and she might have been any woman.

'Duarte...' she framed jerkily as soon as he had replaced the phone. 'I'd like to stay in England—'

'That's not possible unless you insist on a divorce.'

Emily did not feel that she was in a position to insist on anything. Duarte had slaughtered all the protest in her the very instant he had threatened to fight her for custody of Jamie. She'd already spent far too many months fretting about how poor a parent she might seem in comparison to him in any courtroom. Her evident lapse in fidelity, her flight to England, her fear-inspired failure to deal with matters like an adult which had forced Duarte to mount a search. Nothing that she had so far done would impress a judge. Nor would her case be helped when it came out that she had been raising Jamie in a caravan while she roved around taking casual employment. In a Portuguese court, she had not the slightest doubt that Duarte would win custody of their child.

She curved her trembling hands together to steady them. 'I thought you would want a divorce.'

'Not at present.'

Emily wanted to scream. He was shutting her out. He had always done that, depersonalising every encounter, holding her at a distance...except in bed. Her fair complexion reddened to ferocious heat at that inadvertent thought. Just then, she could not bear to recall the physical intimacy which she had once cherished as evidence that he must care for her to some degree. Now it pained her to recall her own humiliating naivety. They had had separate bedrooms from the start. Sex had always seemed to have a faint aura of the forbidden. But it also had been wildly exciting...for *her*. The only time she had dared to touch him had been in the privacy of her own bed. In daylight, Duarte had been way too intimidating.

In a fierce struggle to control her wayward mind, Emily made herself focus on the child's car seat anchored opposite. Jamie's seat. Duarte was taking them both back to Portugal. Duarte was not thinking of a divorce. Duarte was not currently planning to deprive her of her son. Those facts were the *only* facts that mattered right now, she told herself urgently. She was tired of running and exhausted by living on her nerves. All these months, she had had no real life. What lay ahead could surely be little worse than what she had experienced in the past...

'Are you going to have other women...again?' Emily heard herself ask and almost died on the spot because that dreadful question had just come out of nowhere and leapt on to her unguarded tongue.

The silence seemed to flex like a stranglehold ready to tighten round her slender throat.

Slowly, Emily looked up, aquamarine eyes aghast.

Duarte gazed back at her as if she had just dropped down through the car roof, a fully fledged alien with two heads. 'What do you mean by...*again*?' he prompted very softly.

Emily connected with electrifying dark golden eyes and gulped. 'I didn't mean anything...I...I just wondered.'

'You made an accusation,' Duarte contradicted with razor-edged cool. 'A specious feminine attempt to justify your own behaviour by implying that *I* played away—'

Emily was backtracking so fast she was literally into full-throttle reverse. Not because she was a coward but because she could not afford to antagonise Duarte, lest he change his mind and decide that Jamie did not need his mother as much as he believed he did. 'No, I didn't...I didn't—'

'Don't try it again,' Duarte warned steadily, shimmering eyes resting on her like a slowly uncoiling whip lash.

Turning away in turmoil to stare fixedly into the middle distance, Emily only then appreciated that the car had already pulled up outside Alice's farmhouse. The chauffeur opened the passenger door and she leapt out like a rabbit with a fox on her tail. The older woman was already coming outside with Jamie clasped in her arms. 'Will you and Duarte join me for coffee?'

Emily reclaimed Jamie, her heart beating very fast. She didn't want to get back into the limo. She wanted to run again and she knew that this time there was no place to run. 'I'll ask Duarte if we've got time—'

But Duarte was right behind her. He greeted Alice with a courteous charm which Emily had only got to enjoy briefly during their even more brief courtship. Emily stared at her husband, marvelling at the tone of regret he contrived to employ as he refused an invitation he could not have had the slightest desire to accept. She said goodbye in a dulled little voice and got back into the car to fix Jamie into his seat.

'Stop cringing around me,' Duarte instructed grittily as the chauffeur closed the door on them again.

At least the previous unfortunate subject which she had opened was forgotten. But she noted that he had given her no answer. Not that she cared any more, she told herself. They would hardly be living together again but wasn't it peculiar that he wasn't talking about what they were going to be doing? Or was exerting that kind of power over her part of the punishment?

Becoming only slowly aware of the silence, Emily turned her head. Only then did she recall that Duarte was really only now having his first meeting with his son. Duarte was studying Jamie with an intensity she could feel. Jamie was kicking his feet, smiling and in the mood to be admired. Emily watched Duarte. The tension etched in his bold bronzed features, the movement of the lean brown hand he semi-raised and then settled back on a long powerful thigh again.

He wanted to touch Jamie. He wanted to connect; naturally he did. Her throat thickened in the weighted quiet. She slid Jamie's little blue teddy towards Duarte, nudging his braced fingers with the toy. 'You could give him that—'

'When I need your advice, I'll ask for it.' Lean strong face clenching hard, Duarte dealt her a flaring glance of bitter hostility. 'It's not a lot of fun wondering whether my own child will scream if I try to touch him.'

Emily paled. 'I know…I'm sorry—'

A tiny muscle pulling tight at the corner of his hard jaw-line, Duarte thrust his broad shoulders back against the seat.

'I've got plenty of time to get to know him. I'll do it without an audience.'

He was so incredibly proud. Had she not seen the yearning in Duarte's body language as he contemplated his infant son, she might have believed that he felt nothing.

'I was scared to get in contact with you…I was scared of losing him—'

'I'm not about to discuss your behaviour in front of him. You're his mother. You sound distressed. Look at your son…he's listening to your voice and watching your every move and you're *scaring* him,' Duarte condemned.

Emily saw the truth of that censure in Jamie's anxious air and her strained eyes stung, forcing her to blink rapidly. She compressed her lips on all the words that wanted to spill out of her but which Duarte did not want to hear. And could she really blame him? She *was* making excuses again. Right at that moment, Duarte's sole interest was in his son. She was just an adjunct, along for the ride because Jamie needed her. However, it was painfully obvious to Emily that Duarte was barely tolerating her presence.

From the instant they entered the crowded bustling airport, Emily became conscious of her scuffed shoes, faded jodhpurs and ancient sweater. The outfit had been practical for the long drive she had expected to have but she felt like a tramp beside Duarte, immaculate in a charcoal grey suit exquisitely tailored to his tall athletic physique.

'I could have done with getting changed,' she said uneasily. 'But I don't really have anything suitable.'

She had left all her expensive clothes behind in Portugal. Not that that much mattered, she conceded ruefully, for that wardrobe had rejoiced most in fashion accidents. If she got the colour right, she invariably got the style wrong. Growing up, she had been a tomboy, living in jeans and riding gear. Her attempt to experiment with a more feminine look had been squashed in her sensitive teens by her

sisters' scorn. It had been poor preparation for marriage to
a rich man and entry into a daunting world in which her
appearance really seemed to matter.

'You can buy an outfit here and change,' Duarte pointed
out.

To Emily those words were confirmation that she looked
an embarrassing mess. Her throat thickened and her eyes
stung and she reddened fiercely for she had no money either. She hovered over Jamie's buggy with a downbent
head.

Through swimming eyes, Emily focused on the gold
credit card extended in silence by her husband. The most
enormous bitterness and pain seemingly rose out of nowhere inside her and she whispered helplessly, 'You
should've married some fancy model, a real fashion
plate...not someone like me!'

'It is a little late now.' Duarte's deflating tone was more
than equal to capping even the most emotional outburst.
'And this is not the place to stage an argument.'

Emily swallowed hard. When had she ever had the nerve
to argue with him? Yet it was odd how much she now
wanted to argue but she was far too conscious of being in
public where angry words would be overheard. Accepting
the credit card without looking at him, she released her hold
on the buggy and headed for the closest dress shop. There
she scanned the packed displays. Choose really bright colours, Bliss had once advised Emily, saying that such shades
flattered Emily's pale skin tone and balanced her red hair.
Emily sped over to a rack of cerise dresses but they were
way too plain in design to conceal a figure that Bliss had
gently pointed out was more boyish than lush. Browsing at
speed, she picked a jazzy orange handkerchief top with bell
sleeves and a big glittery lime green motif on the front.
Nobody was likely to notice her lack in the bosom depart-

ment under that, Emily thought gratefully. She teamed the top with a long orange skirt that had the same fancy hem.

Both garments matched in colour and style, she reflected with relief, thinking that that should definitely ensure a presentable appearance. She picked up a pair of high-heeled leopard-print mules because she knew they were the height of fashion. Her purchases made, she made harried use of a changing cubicle. Emerging from the shop again, hot and breathless, she saw Duarte and his security men standing around Jamie's buggy in the centre of the wide concourse.

Mateus and the rest of his team focused on her and momentarily stared before lowering their heads. Then Duarte glanced in her direction and froze. Not a single betraying expression appeared on his darkly handsome features but he seemed to breathe in very deep and slow. And she knew right then that she had got it wrong again. Her heart sank right down to the toes of her horribly uncomfortable mules and she despised herself for her own weakness, her pathetic attempt to please and win his approval in even the smallest way.

'Sorry I took so long,' she mumbled, reclaiming the buggy without glancing back up at him but conscious of his brooding presence with every fibre of her wretched being.

'No...problem,' Duarte sighed.

In the VIP lounge, she caught an involuntary glimpse of herself in a mirror and she was startled. She looked like a fluorescent carrot, she decided in stricken recoil. Flinching, she turned away from that mortifying reflection. Sitting down, she tried to disappear into herself and her own thoughts in the manner she had begun to practise within months of marrying Duarte. He never had been any great fan of idle chatter. She just wanted to sink into the woodwork, sitting there in an outfit that he most probably thought was ghastly. So why did she care? Why did she *still* care?

Emily had always been conscious that she was neither pretty nor beautiful. Her mother and both her sisters were tall shapely blondes with classic bone structures. Even in appearance, she had not fitted her family. At the age of ten, she had asked her mother where her own red hair came from in the family tree as even her father was fair. Her mother had dealt her a angry look as if even asking such a question was offensive and had told her that she owed her 'unfortunate' carroty curls to the genetic legacy of her late grandmother.

Seeing no point in bemoaning what could not be altered, Emily hadn't ever really minded being short, red-haired and small in the chest and hip department. But the same moment that she first saw Duarte Avila de Monteiro, she had started minding very much that she would never have what it would take to attract him. Of course, it had not once occurred to her that a male of his calibre and wealth would look twice at her anyway but she still remembered her own foolish feelings of intense sadness and hurt that it should be that way. That Duarte should be so utterly detached from her when her own senses thrilled to even his presence a hundred feet away.

And she still recalled the very first moment she had laid eyes on Duarte and very much doubted that *he* did...

CHAPTER THREE

BY THE time she was nineteen, Emily had qualified as a riding instructor.

Her two older sisters had found lucrative employment in their father's wine-importing business but Emily had not been offered the same opportunity. Indeed, urged by her mother to leave home and be independent long before she was earning enough to pay a decent rent, Emily had finally given up on the job she loved. She had taken work as a live-in groom at Ash Manor, Duarte's English country house.

The stable manager had hired Emily and, working at the manor, she had had an interesting insight into the lifestyle of a super-rich and powerful banker. Aside from his private jet, his fleet of helicopters and luxury cars, Duarte owned half a dozen palatial homes, superb horseflesh and a priceless art collection. He was the guy with everything, the target of endless awe, speculation and envy. But the one thing Duarte Avila de Monteiro did not have, it seemed, was the precious *time* to enjoy his innumerable possessions.

It had been weeks before Emily actually saw her wealthy employer in the flesh but she had already been told what he was like. Cool, polite, distant, formal, not the type to unbend with lesser beings, very much the product of a Portuguese aristocratic lineage said to stretch back to the thirteenth century.

His incredible silver sports car pulled up one afternoon while Emily and another female groom were cleaning tack. The stable manager hurried from his office to greet Duarte. 'That car's a MacLaren F1, worth six hundred grand,'

Emily's companion groaned. 'And just wait until you see *him*. When I first came here, I assumed the banker boss was some old geezer, but he's only twenty-eight and he's pure sex on legs. If you got him on his own without his bodyguards, you'd lock him in your bedroom and throw away the key!'

Even more than two years on, Emily still remembered that first shattering sight of Duarte. Sunlight gleaming over the luxuriant black hair stylishly cropped to his proud head as he climbed out of his car, a crisp white shirt accentuating his bronzed complexion but most of all she had noticed his stunning eyes, deepset and dark as sable at first glance but tawny gold as a hunting animal's the next. She was shocked and bemused by the unfamiliar leap of her own senses and the quite ridiculous stab of loss which assailed her when he turned away to open the passenger door of his car.

In place of the beautiful woman she had expected to see in Duarte's passenger seat was an absolutely huge shaggy dog curled up nose to tail into the smallest possible size.

The other groom backed into the tack out of sight. 'I'm not going to get stuck with that monster again. That dog's as thick as a block of wood, won't come when you call it and it's as fast on its feet as a race horse!'

Before the other girl even finished speaking, the stable manager called Emily over and told her to exercise the dog.

It was an Irish wolfhound. Unfolded from the car, it had to measure a good three feet in height and Emily was just one inch over five feet tall herself. But although Emily had not been allowed to have a pet as a child, she adored dogs of all shapes and sizes.

'Be kind. Jazz is getting old,' Duarte's rich, dark, accented drawl interposed with cool authority.

Emily angled a shy upward glance at him, overwhelmed by his proximity, his sheer height and breadth and potent masculinity. She had to tip her head right back to see his

lean, dark, devastating face. She collided with sizzling dark
golden eyes and for her it was like being knocked off her
feet by a powerful electrical charge. She trembled, felt the
feverish heat of an embarrassing blush redden her fair skin,
the stormy thump of her heartbeat and the most challenging
shortness of breath. But Duarte simply walked away from
her again, apparently experiencing no physical jolt of
awareness, feeling nothing whatsoever, indeed not really
even having seen her for she had only been another junior
employee amongst many: faceless, beneath his personal notice.

And, no doubt, had not fate intervened, her acquaintance
with Duarte Avila de Monteiro would never have advanced
beyond that point. However, in those days, Duarte had left
Jazz behind at the manor when he was out of the country.
The dog should have stayed indoors but the housekeeper
had disliked animals and as soon as Duarte departed, she
would have the wolfhound locked in the barn. Exercising
Jazz fell to Emily for nobody else wanted the responsibility.

'The boss is fond of that stupid dog. If it gets lost or
harmed in some way, well it'll cost you your job,' the stable
manager warned Emily impatiently. 'That's why we just
leave it locked up. I know it seems a little heartless but the
animal's well fed and it has plenty of space in there.'

But Emily was too tender-hearted to bear the sound of
Jazz's pathetic cries for company. She spent all her free
time playing with him in a paddock and she gave him the
affection he soaked up like a giant hungry sponge. So, the
evening that the barn went up in fire, when everyone else
stood by watching the growing conflagration in horror,
Emily did not even stop to think of her own safety but
charged to the rescue of an animal she had grown to love.

Although she contrived to calm Jazz's panic and persuade him out of the barn, she passed out soon afterwards
from smoke inhalation. Surfacing from the worst effects,

she then found herself in a private room in the local hospital with Duarte stationed by her bedside.

The instant she opened her eyes, Duarte sprang up and approached the bed, his appearance startling her out of what remained of her scrambled wits. 'Risking your own life to save my dog was incredibly foolish *and* incredibly brave,' he murmured with a reflective smile that in spite of its haunting brevity had more charm than she had believed any smile might possess.

'I just didn't think,' she mumbled, transfixed by the drop-dead gorgeous effect of him smiling.

'You are a heroine. I contacted your family.' His strong jawline squared. 'I understand that they are very busy people and, of course, I told them that you were already recovering. I am not sure whether or not they will find it possible to visit.'

Paling at that sympathetic rendering of her family's evident lack of concern at the news that she had been hospitalised, Emily veiled her pained gaze. 'Thanks…'

'It is I who am in debt to you. One of the grooms had the courage to confess that, but for you, Jazz would have spent every hour of my absence imprisoned in that barn,' Duarte admitted grimly. 'You are the only one in a staff of almost twenty who had the kindness to take care of his needs.'

Embarrassed by that unsought accolade, Emily muttered, 'I just like animals and Jazz may be a bit daft but he's very loving.'

The forbidding look on his lean dark features dissipated and he vented a rueful laugh. 'Jazz has a brain the size of a pea. He was my sister's dog. After her death, he should have been rehomed but I did not have the heart to part with him.' His face shadowed again. 'Perhaps that was a selfish decision for I am often away on business—'

'No. He just adores you. I couldn't get him to settle at

night until I got the housekeeper to give me an old sweater of yours to put in his bed,' Emily volunteered in a rush.

There was an awkward little silence. Faint colour now scored his superb cheekbones. He studied her through black lashes lush as silk fans, palpably questioning why he had unbent to such an extent with her. A minute later, he had been the powerful banker again, politely taking his departure, having done his duty in visiting her. A magnificent bouquet of flowers and a basket of fruit had been delivered soon after his departure. She had not expected to see him again except at a distance when he was at the manor.

But the next day when she was released from hospital, Duarte picked her up and insisted on driving her home to convalesce with her family. She spent the whole journey falling deeper and deeper in love with a guy so out of her reach he might as well have come from another galaxy. There was only a little conversation during that drive for Duarte was often on the phone.

Her family took one astonished but thrilled look at Duarte and his chauffeur-driven limousine and invited him to stay to dinner. Billionaire single bankers were hugely welcome in a house containing two young, beautiful single blondes. Indeed, her sisters Hermione and Corinne had competed for Duarte's attention with outrageous flattery and provocative innuendoes. Sunk in the background as usual by their flirtatious charm, Emily had felt painfully like the ugly duckling amongst the swans.

Emily was sprung back to the present by the necessity of boarding the jet. Soon after take-off, she realised that Jamie was overtired and cross. The steward showed her into a rear compartment where a special travel cot already waited in readiness for its small occupant. It took Emily a good twenty minutes to settle Jamie and then, with pronounced reluctance, she returned to the luxurious main cabin again.

Duarte rose from his seat and straightened to his full commanding height. 'Is Jamie asleep?'

Emily nodded jerkily, her tension rising by the second.

'Verbal responses would be welcome,' Duarte added drily.

Encountering brilliant dark golden eyes, she reddened hotly. 'Yes, he's asleep but maybe I should sit with him for a while in case he wakes up again.'

'Trying to impress me with maternal overkill? Tell me, who looked after Jamie while you were giving riding lessons?'

'Nobody—'

'*Nobody?*' Duarte queried with hard emphasis.

Emily frowned in surprise. 'It really wasn't a problem. I was only instructing a couple of hours a day and I would park Jamie's buggy outside the paddock. He was never more than a few feet from me and he usually had the company of parents watching their child's lesson.'

As Duarte listened, his lean powerful face tautened, his wide sensual mouth compressing. 'Usually? A working stables is no place to leave a baby unattended. You know as well as I do that riders can't always control their mounts and that your attention must've been on your pupil—'

Under that attack, Emily had stiffened and lost much of her natural colour. 'Jamie was always safe. I did the very best that I could—'

'But your best wasn't halfway good enough,' Duarte cut in with biting derision. 'You left my son at the mercy of passing strangers instead of ensuring that he received proper care—'

'I wanted to spend every minute with him that I could and you're making this sound much worse than it was,' Emily protested defensively. 'Everywhere I worked, Jamie got loads and loads of attention. Most people like babies, especially happy ones—'

'That's not the point,' Duarte said coldly.

Emily worried at her lower lip and then said heavily, 'Even if I had wanted to, I couldn't have afforded to pay someone to look after him—'

'And whose fault was that?'

As her tension climbed, Emily trembled and her tummy churned. Thinking straight had become a challenge; she had never been much good at confrontations. However, on this occasion she found herself struggling to speak up in her own defence. 'Whose fault was it that I left Portugal in the first place?'

Far from looking impressed or indeed startled by that comeback, Duarte inclined his arrogant dark head to one side and levelled his incisive gaze on her in the most formidable way. 'Presumably you are about to give me the answer to that strange question?' he prompted.

'I only left Portugal because I thought that you were planning to try and take my child off me the minute he was born!' Emily countered in an accusing rush.

Duarte angled an imperious brow. 'What kind of a nonsensical excuse is that? Before this morning, I never made a threat in that line. To be frank, my patience with you came to an end today. But who or what gave you the idea that I might have been considering such a dramatic move last year?'

Emily flinched and dropped her head, shaken at how close she had come in her turmoil to revealing Bliss's role in events eight months earlier. Had she done that, she could never have forgiven herself. Bliss had been the truest of supportive friends during Emily's troubled marriage, cheering Emily up when her spirits were low while offering helpful advice and encouragement. Although Emily had not contacted the other woman since leaving Portugal, she assumed that her friend still worked as Duarte's executive assistant. Bliss had eavesdropped on that confidential dia-

logue between Duarte and his lawyer and had forewarned
Emily. Were Duarte ever to discover that a member of his
own staff had been that disloyal, Bliss's high-flying career
would be destroyed.

'I just got the idea…at the time, the way you were treating me—well, er…it seemed to make sense to me and I
was afraid that you were planning to separate me from my
child—'

'So you chose to separate our son from *me* instead. Is
that how this sorry story goes?' Duarte dealt her a look of
shimmering challenge that made her breath trip in her already tight throat. 'This convenient angle that continually
seeks to turn you into a poor little victim? Well, I have
news for you—I'm not impressed, *querida*.'

'I'm not trying to impress—'

'No?' Without warning, Duarte sent her a sudden slanting golden glance as hard and deadly as an arrow thudding
into a live target.

Feeling the sudden smouldering surge in the atmosphere
but unable to comprehend what had caused it, Emily un-
twisted her laced hands and made a jerky move with one
of them as if she was appealing for his attention. 'I know
I've made mistakes—'

'Mistakes?'

'—but now I'm just being open and honest—'

'*Open*…and *honest*,' Duarte repeated with a brand of
electrifying soft sibilance that danced down her rigid spine
like a fullscale storm warning. '*Que absurdo!* An honest
whore you were not!'

Emily's lips parted company and she fell back a faltering
step in dismay at the proclamation and that particular word
being aimed at her. Even in the aftermath of finding her in
another man's arms, Duarte had not employed such an
emotive term. 'B-but—'

'But what? You were carrying my baby when you slept

with another man. How many women have affairs while they're pregnant with their husband's child?' Duarte demanded in a derisive tone of disgust that nailed her to the spot. 'But no such fine sensibilities restrained *you*. You even dared to introduce me to your lover. You also brought him into my home. Only a whore would behave like that.'

Forced to recognise the extent of the sins being laid at her door, Emily gasped strickenly, 'Duarte, it wasn't like that and Toby was *never* my—'

'Do you really think I'll listen to your pathetic excuses? You are nothing to me.' Duarte made that wounding statement with a savage cool that bled all remaining colour from her shaken face.

You are nothing to me. That he should feel that way was hardly news but spoken out loud that acknowledgement cut Emily in two.

'But you belong to me. *Minha esposa*…you are my wife,' Duarte completed with sardonic bite.

Under the onslaught of that ultimate putdown, Emily felt something curiously akin to a re-energising flame dart through her slim tense body and she flung her head back. 'No…I don't belong to you like your cars and your houses and your wretched art collection,' she heard herself asserting. 'I may be your wife but I'm not an object without any thoughts or feelings or rights—'

Although she had no recollection of him moving, Duarte was now a step closer, threateningly close. Even as she was still fighting to understand quite where her own unusually spirited defence had come from, she was awesomely conscious of the expanse of all that lean, taut masculinity poised within inches of her own much smaller frame.

In the electrifying silence that had fallen, shimmering golden eyes sought and held her scrutiny, all the powerful force of will he possessed bearing down on her. 'You have no rights in this marriage.'

'I don't believe you mean that...you couldn't,' Emily reasoned, tearing her gaze hurriedly from his as her heart rate speeded up. 'You're just very angry with me—'

'I am not angry with you,' Duarte growled like a leopard about to spring on an unwary prey. 'But I cannot and will not trust you with the kind of freedom I gave you before.'

'*That*...was freedom?' A startled laugh empty of humour was wrenched from Emily's working throat, for she had found her duties as a Monteiro wife as rigid a constraint to her days as a prison cell. Every daylight hour had been rigorously organised for her with a weighty yoke of responsibilities that took no account of her own personal wishes.

Hard dark colour scored the hard set of Duarte's proud cheekbones. 'So you find my former generosity a source of amusement?'

'Oh, you mean your money...' Emily very nearly let loose a second nervous laugh as comprehension finally sank in and her soft mouth tensed. 'Well, it wasn't much consolation when you were never around and I never did take to shopping, although I did try hard to like it. You see, I wasn't the sort of woman you should have married and I still can't really understand why you *did*...'

Duarte stared down at her with eyes as dark and fathomless and deep as the midnight witching hour. As he ensnared her fraught gaze afresh, she forgot what she was saying at the same time as she forgot to draw another breath. The atmosphere surged around her like a slow smouldering fire closing in, using up all the oxygen. But still she stood there, plunged without warning into a welter of physical sensations she had never been able to fight. As a wave of excitement as terrifying as it was thrilling washed over her, her heart thumped like a frantic bird trapped inside her, every tiny muscle tensing in reaction to the rush of liquid heat burning between her slim thighs.

'Can't you?' he murmured huskily.

The very sound of that silken dark drawl sent a responsive shiver down her spine. She snatched in a stark audible breath to flood her depleted lungs. She was tormentingly aware of the stirring heaviness of her small breasts and the painful sensitivity of her swollen nipples pushing against the bra she wore beneath her top.

'Aside from my wealth, I had nothing to offer you but you appeared to want very little.' Duarte studied her with spectacular dark golden eyes that had the most scorching effect on her already heated flesh. 'Apart from me…and you wanted me like you wanted air to breathe. At the time it seemed a fair exchange.'

Her mind a mess of jumbled and inane thoughts, Emily quivered as she literally struggled to concentrate on what he had just said. Understanding came in a trickle and then a gush and almost washed her away in a floodtide of pain and humiliation. Like an accident victim, she reeled back a step from their proximity, aquamarine eyes shattered, shame over her own weakness where he was concerned following fast.

You wanted me like you wanted air to breathe…

It was the most hurtful but demeaning truth she had ever had to swallow. Momentarily it threw her back into the past and a time when she would have done anything, accepted anything on any terms just to be with him. And all this time *he* had known that, a little voice of horror wailed inside her head. She was appalled and then shaken by her own refusal to accept that he had recognised from the very outset just how deep his hold over her was. All the shameless heat he had awakened without even trying drained away, only to be replaced by a fiery surge of hot colour that dwindled equally fast.

'You shouldn't have asked,' Duarte murmured, smooth as glass.

'Once…you wouldn't have answered,' Emily parted numb lips to respond and her own voice emerged all bumpy and broken.

'That was then. This is now and much has changed.' Duarte surveyed her with hard dark eyes of satisfaction. 'But, sadly for you, not, I think, your hunger for me.'

'Well, that's where you're dead wrong…' A sudden re-vivifying burst of bitter anger powered through Emily's quivering length. 'As you said, that was then and this is *now* and I got over my stupid crush when you got me pregnant and then decided to forget I even existed!'

'Did you really get over it?' Duarte reached for her with such a complete lack of warning and such shattering cool that she stared up at him in a wide-eyed daze, a frown just beginning to form between her brows. Before she even had the chance to blink, his hard sensual mouth came down on hers with all the explosive force and expertise of a heat-seeking missile.

Since that onslaught was the very last reaction she'd expected, she had no time to even try to muster her defences. She was blasted from angry shame straight into stunned and helpless response, a muffled gasp torn from her throat as he crushed her into the steely contours of his hard powerful physique. She couldn't breathe, didn't want to, couldn't think, didn't want to. Her whole body seemed to surge up and into his, instantly fired by the burning heat of desire he could unleash. He pried her lips apart, let his tongue delve in carnal and provocative exploration of the tender interior of her mouth and she shuddered and moaned as the upswell of electrifying sensation became more than she could bear.

'Duarte…' she gasped feverishly. 'Duarte—'

'Jamie's crying. You should go to him.'

Like a woman lost in a dream she let him set her back from him. Her brain felt befogged and her body was still gripped in the talon claws of an excitement she had never expected to feel again.

'Jamie…' Duarte said again.

And, in the same instant, her wits returned and she emerged from the grasp of the sensual world which had betrayed her with a sudden nasty jolt. Blinking rapidly, she pressed a trembling hand to the tiny pulse flickering like mad above her collarbone and she stared up at Duarte in resounding shock. His lean, dark, devastating face was cool as ice, his brilliant dark golden eyes challenging.

Jamie! Finally recognising the faint cry that she normally reacted to within seconds, Emily hurried away, pale as death and all knotted up inside with maternal guilt and self-loathing. Jamie had mislaid his teddy but he calmed down the instant his mother reappeared. The teddy restored to his grasping hand, his sleepy brown eyes pinned to her face and then slowly began to drift closed again. Emily sat down on the bed by the cot.

She was still trembling and her body ached from that elemental surge of hunger which she suppressed for so long. Of course, it had been so much easier to deny that side of her nature when Duarte was not around. Reliving the immediacy with which she had fallen into his arms, she squirmed and hated herself. She should have had more pride. But on another level she was simply stunned that Duarte should actually have *touched* her again. Duarte who, eleven months ago, had said he could not even stand for her to remain beneath the same roof.

Yet, he had touched her again and she had made a fool of herself. But then, she ought to be used to that by now, she conceded heavily. Hadn't her gorgeous sophisticated husband always specialised in running rings around her besotted self? And her mind slid back again into the past when just a glimpse of Duarte had lit up her world…

A month after the fire in the barn, Emily had been informed that Duarte wanted to see her. Fresh from the morning exercise run with the horses, Emily had been cringingly conscious of her messy hair and muddy clothing but too worried about *why* he should want to see her to waste time getting changed.

For the first time, she set foot *inside* Ash Manor to see the beautifully restored Georgian interior that lay beyond the imposing front door. Jazz raced across the hall to throw himself at her with his usual exuberance. She got down on the floor to give him a hug that turned into a mock wrestling session—and then discovered that Duarte was standing watching her childish antics with his dog.

Momentarily his rare smile glimmered on his lips and he said something but she didn't catch what he said. The visual effect of Duarte after four weeks of deprivation had bereft her of all rational thought and concentration. In strong embarrassment, she'd scrambled up and he had shown her into a library where he invited her to sit down.

'I'm pretty dirty.' Emily had scanned the watered silk covering the indicated chair, preferring to look at it rather than at him as her wretched face burned scarlet. 'I'd be better standing.'

'As you wish. I won't be keeping you long.' Duarte lounged back against a polished desk, the very picture of polished elegance in his tailored business suit. 'When I entertain here, my friends and business associates often bring their families with them. I believe you're a riding instructor. I'd like you to start giving lessons to my younger guests. Naturally I'll raise your salary. Are you interested?'

Emily glanced up with a surprised but pleased smile. 'Very much.'

That winter, Duarte spent a remarkable amount of time at Ash Manor. Her duties gradually extended to generally supervising and entertaining any visiting children. At the end of the first month, Duarte said that it would be more convenient if she moved out of the flat she shared with the other grooms and into the manor itself. Dismayed to then be told that she was expected to take her meals in the dining room, she had ducked that challenge on the first night. Settling down to her evening meal in the kitchen, she had been aghast when Duarte strode in.

'What are you doing in here?' he had demanded in exasperation, startling her half out of her wits. 'You eat with my guests now.'

But everyone but Duarte and the children had ignored her in the dining room. Content to be ignored in a gathering of so many wealthy and important people, she had been taken aback when Duarte continually attempted to drag her into conversations.

'I heard Mr Monteiro tell Mum that you're marvellous with children and animals,' one of her temporary charges told her chattily one rainy evening while they worked on a horribly complex jigsaw. 'And very kind... Can I stay up until we finish this?'

Crumbs to a starving heart, she'd thought at the time, hugging those few words of approval to herself but secretly wishing that those words had been more personal. But much much later, when she was Duarte's wife, she had finally grasped that she had been under observation during that period, marched out like a reluctant-to-perform animal so that he could see how she behaved, how she thought, how she reacted in different situations. And quiet and shy had ultimately been fine with him. After all, what qualities does a male look for in a low-maintenance wife?

For that was the starring role for which she had been carefully picked with the minimum of required effort on his part. A low-maintenance wife, dead keen on soppy things like kids and dogs, unlikely to require much attention.

'You've done a terrific job,' Duarte informed her some weeks later. 'Let me take you out to dinner.'

Paralysed to the spot, she had stared at him. 'Oh, there's no need for that—'

'Emily—'

'Really, I wouldn't be comfortable imposing on you like that,' she had gabbled, distressed and embarrassed at the idea that he believed that he owed her some sort of treat for admittedly working very long hours.

'But I insist. Dinner… Eight,' Duarte had stated curtly.

So he took her out to dinner and she sat looking at him like a hypnotised rabbit, mumbling responses, spilling her wine and, due to the fancy menu couched in French, ending up with raw steak when what she had really wanted was a well-done one.

'Why are you so nervous?' he had finally asked with an air of imperturbable calm that just might have been laced with concealed exasperation.

'I'm just not comfortable,' she told him miserably.

'But we have often talked before this.'

'This is different—'

'So it is…' Duarte had given her a wry look. 'I don't believe I've had a date this disastrous since I was a teenager.'

'A…a *date*?' she had stressed in considerable shock.

'Why not? I like you, Emily. What more is required?'

After marrying him, she could have told him exactly what was required. But that evening, offered the substance of her wildest fantasies she had had no such caution and commonsense. She had simply gazed back at him, transfixed by a sensation of wondering joy and gratitude. 'I like you too,' she'd said inanely.

'Excellent,' Duarte had pronounced as the plate of raw steak was discreetly removed at his instruction to be replaced some timeless period later by a cooked one.

'In fact, I like you a lot,' Emily had heard herself adding like an eager schoolgirl.

'Even better,' Duarte had asserted valiantly.

But he hadn't kissed her that week or the next. In fact if she hadn't hovered one night during the third week in the most humiliatingly suggestive way, she honestly believed that he might not have bothered to kiss her at all until he married her. Evidently registering that some lusty enthusiasm was required to impress even the most shy and inexperienced of women, he had got it all over with at once. He had taken her to bed the same night. In the dawn hours, while she was lying on the far side of the bed, wondering frantically whether she ought to be sneaking back to her own room, Duarte had opened his stunning dark golden eyes and rested them on her blushing face and murmured with grave quietness, 'Will you marry me, Emily?'

And she had not asked why. Nor had she or he broached a single one of the questions that she imagined people usually exchanged on such a momentous occasion. She'd just nodded like a marionette having her strings pulled by expert hands. And those expert hands had reached for her again in reality as he breathed lazily, 'I may already have got you pregnant. We'll get married very soon.'

Emily was sprung from her introspection by an announcement over the tannoy that the jet was soon to land. With a groan at the necessity, she lifted her sleeping son from the cot and returned to the main cabin.

CHAPTER FOUR

WHEN Emily emerged from the jet with Jamie in her arms, she saw two limousines waiting on the tarmac to greet them. A slim svelte female, clad in an elegant suit the shade of eau-de-nil alighted from the first car. As the woman's pale golden hair glinted in the evening sunlight, a warm smile relaxed Emily's tense mouth and she hurried down the steps in Duarte's wake.

Bliss was *still* working for Duarte! As Bliss finally spotted Emily and the baby she was carrying, her face froze and she momentarily stilled. Naturally Bliss would be stunned to see her back in Portugal, Emily reflected, and then hurriedly ditched her own smile in an effort to be more discreet. Bliss had said that Duarte would never approve of his wife embarking on a close friendship with one of his personal staff and, naturally, Bliss had not wanted to risk damaging her career prospects.

'Mrs Monteiro...' Bliss acknowledged coolly, her clear blue eyes skimming off Emily just as quickly again, her exquisite face expressionless.

Bliss was being really discreet, Emily decided but she felt just a bit cut off by that greeting and anxiously wondered if she had offended the other woman with her silence in recent months. If she had, it would be ironic for she had stayed out of touch rather than subject her friend to the stress of further divided loyalties.

'Wait in the car, Emily,' Duarte instructed in an arctic tone.

Reddening as Mateus surged ahead of her to open the passenger door of the rear limousine, Emily climbed in and gazed back out at her husband and his executive assistant where they remained about thirty feet away. Duarte looked very grave but, as always, stunningly handsome. All tall and dark and sleek and bronzed, command and authority stamped into every hard line of his lean powerful face. Bliss, who had always reminded Emily of a fairytale princess brought to life, looked curiously frozen and a bright swathe of pink now burned over her delicate cheekbones.

Striding over to the limo, Duarte swung in beside Emily and the car moved off. Surprised that the jet had landed at Lisbon rather than at Oporto, Emily wondered if Duarte was heading to a business meeting. Certain that Duarte intended to send both her and his son back to the house in the Douro, Emily contemplated the very long car journey which lay ahead for her and Jamie.

At least it was spring, she thought ruefully. She had spent the winter of their separation in the country house and it had been dismal. These days the Monteiros only ever used the property for a rustic summer break or during the *vindima*, the grape harvest when the Portuguese enjoyed getting back to their roots. In winter, the villa had been shrouded in the thick grey mists that rose above the dramatic high banks of the Douro river and day after day it had rained heavily and got colder. Emily shivered at those depressing recollections.

'Perhaps I could spend the winters in England,' Emily proposed in a small taut voice.

Duarte moved a lean, silencing hand for he was talking on the car phone. He frowned at her, winged black brows drawing together above clear golden eyes. Biting at her lip, Emily turned away again. The limo had already left the motorway. They were on the outskirts of the pretty hilltown of Sintra and within a startling stone's throw of her former marital home, the Quinta de Monteiro. She assumed that Duarte was being dropped off home first.

Dense forest covered the hills above the ancient winding streets of the tiny village below the *quinta*. The verges of the road were carpeted with a colourful riot of naturalised crocus and scilla blooms. It was beautiful. But gooseflesh rose on Emily's arms as she found herself studying the narrow corner building where Toby had once had his artist's studio. The window shutters now bore a faded 'for rent' notice.

'I assure you that you won't be spending the winters or indeed, any other season in England,' Duarte imparted that news with a gritty edge to his dark deep drawl. 'I could not trust you that far from my sight.'

Emily twisted her head back with a bemused look. 'I beg your pardon?'

'From now on, everywhere you go you will be accompanied,' Duarte murmured.

'Wh-what on earth are you talking about?' Emily stammered as the opulent car glided below the imposing turreted entrance of the Quinta de Monteiro.

'You heard me.' Spectacular golden eyes tough as granite settled on her with unnerving force. 'If you go riding, you will take a groom, and for all other outings, you will have a driver and a bodyguard. At any hour of the day, I will expect to know where you are and what you are doing—'

'But I never went riding in the Douro...' Emily was having huge difficulty in comprehending the necessity for such excessive arrangements and her bewilderment was visible.

'I spend precious little time at our country house,' Duarte said drily. 'I was merely pointing out that there is a price to pay for my generosity in taking you back.'

'Taking me back...' Emily mumbled in repetition. 'Taking me back...*where*?'

'If I did not know you better, I would believe you were drunk,' Duarte delivered a split second before his chauffeur opened the door beside her. 'We will continue this discussion indoors.'

With an enervated flick of her eyes in the direction of the Quinta de Monteiro, a vast sixteenth-century building as monumental and impressive as a castle, Emily repeated uncertainly, 'Indoors? You want me to come inside?'

'No matter how much one might feel like it, one does not leave one's wife to sleep in the car,' Duarte framed with considerable sarcasm.

Emily sat bolt upright, finally pausing to consider that phrase 'taking you back' in a different light. Not just back to Portugal, it seemed, but back to sharing the former marital roof. True, it was an exceptionally large roof, beneath which the most bitter enemies could probably live separate lives, but even so Emily was shattered by the concept. With an effort, she parted her lips, keen to clarify the matter. 'Duarte...I—'

Springing out on to the gravel, he swung back and grasped her hand in an impatient movement to urge her on. 'Come on... Victorine is waiting to welcome us.'

Emily ducked down her head and peered round him in dismay. There stood Victorine like a door sentinel, a middle-aged woman clad from head to toe in unrelieved black, her face set like an ancient Egyptian grave mask. Welcome? Victorine *welcome* the head of the family's unfaithful wife back to the hallowed ground of the Monteiro ancestral home? Was he joking? Even in the early days of their marriage, Duarte's former mother-in-law had been unable to conceal her antipathy towards Emily.

'I'm not going in,' Emily argued in a feverish undertone. 'I had no idea you were bringing us here. I thought I was going back to the house in the Douro—'

'Then a geography lesson would appear to be in order,' Duarte gritted without hesitation. 'Get out of the car, Emily.

For once in your life behave as I might reasonably expect
my wife to behave.'

Every scrap of colour drained from her complexion at
that wounding statement which reminded her of her every
past failure. Then redemption and release came from a new
discovery deep within her pain. 'I'm sorry...I really don't
want to be your wife any more,' she whispered and her
voice might have shook but somehow that admission made
her feel stronger than she had felt in a very long time.

'*Meu Deus!*' Duarte bent down and scooped her out of
the passenger seat with powerful and angry hands. 'That I
should lower myself to the dishonour of taking back an
adulterous wife and that you should *dare* to display such
ingratitude in response!' he growled down at her with enraged golden eyes.

Emily gasped in disbelief when Duarte lifted her bodily
from the car with the ease of a male sweeping up a small
recalcitrant child. She could not credit that her controlled
and reserved husband, who was no fan of public displays,
should behave in such a way while Victorine was watching
them. But then, never had she seen Duarte's anger before,
for he'd not allowed her to see it, and what he'd just said
to her was burned like letters of fire into her memory banks.
'Put me down,' she gasped in stricken recoil but her request
was ignored.

When they were still several feet from the tall front doors
which were spread wide on the huge hall behind her,
Victorine spoke. 'I am sorry to say it but if that trollop
enters the *quinta*, I will leave, Duarte.'

'That would be a great pity,' Duarte murmured without
expression as he lowered Emily down on to the step in front
of him. 'But this is my home and within my home no one
will tell me what I may or may not do, nor will anyone
abuse my wife.'

Emily was as shattered by that tough comeback from

Duarte as the older woman appeared to be. Victorine's thin features betrayed incredulous resentment.

'Duarte…' Emily began in an agony of discomfiture.

'If my daughter Izabel could see you now with *her*…' Victorine condemned with a bitterness she could not hide.

Every muscle in Duarte's big powerful body went rigid and his dark deep voice carried an edge of reproach. 'Let your daughter rest in peace.'

As Victorine stalked back indoors in high dudgeon, it was Emily who broke the strained silence that she had left in her wake. 'Jamie's still in the car—'

'He's asleep. The staff will see to him for the moment.' Signalling the housekeeper hovering at the back of the hall, Duarte gave an instruction to that effect. Then, resting a hand to Emily's taut spine, he pressed her into the superb salon with its tall gothic windows and thrust the door shut behind them again.

The wall at the foot of the room was dominated by a huge full-length portrait of Izabel, an exotic brunette in a fabulous blue ball gown. Emily tore her gaze from that familiar but oh, so daunting image. Izabel, Victorine's beloved only child and Duarte's first wife. Five years earlier, Izabel had died in a ghastly car wreck that had also claimed the life of Duarte's twin sister. *Rest in peace?* Emily's sensitive tummy clenched. One way or another, she had been haunted every day of their marriage by Izabel, the ultimate of impossible acts to follow. Even now, Duarte could not bear to mention her name and the Quinta de Monteiro remained stamped by the spectral presence of its former mistress.

'Please go and speak to Victorine before she does anything foolish,' Emily urged wearily. 'I don't want to stay here anyway, so there's not much point giving her the impression that she has to move out to avoid me.'

'This is my home. Here you will stay.'

That abrasive intonation made her lift her head again and she clashed with smouldering dark golden eyes that could have splintered a lesser being at a hundred paces. She gulped. 'I *can't*... If that's how Victorine feels, what about the rest of the family and your friends?'

Duarte flung back his arrogant head and vented a harsh laugh of derision that ripped through the tense atmosphere like a knife blade. '*Inferno!* Do you think I took out a full page ad in the newspapers to spread the word that the village layabout had been screwing my wife?'

White as milk, Emily stared back at him and cringed. He'd never used such language around her before but in its use she finally recognised the savage anger he was containing and she quailed from it. 'But I never slept with him,' she argued in desperation. 'All that *ever* happened between us, you saw for yourself—'

'Saw and will never forget.' Duarte swore with a raw force that chilled her. 'Don't insult my intelligence. While you were in the Douro, I was foolish enough to reconsider your explanations—but then I received confirmation of your guilt from a third party. It was not *only* I who saw you acting like a slut.'

Emily had backed away several steps. Rigid with stress, she could not stop trembling. 'What third party? How could there be a third party who witnessed something that *never* happened?' she exclaimed in appalled protest. 'Was it your mother-in-law? I don't think Victorine would lose much sleep over lying about me.'

'You wrong her.' Duarte's contempt at that suggestion was unconcealed. 'She may not like you but she was not involved. Nor is your sordid affair common knowledge. Fortunately, that third party I mentioned is not a gossip.'

Emily lifted unsteady hands to her drawn face. It was a warm evening but her skin felt like ice and she dimly registered that she was suffering from the effects of shock. She was devastated to learn that, during their separation eight months earlier, Duarte had been fair enough to think over afresh whether or not she might have been telling the truth about Toby. Then, sadly, he had had his mind made up for him by some hateful person, who had either lied or seriously misinterpreted something they had seen. But who?

But just as suddenly the identity of that mysterious third party no longer seemed of immediate importance to Emily. She had let Toby kiss her and it was little wonder that, having seen that display, Duarte should have no faith whatsoever in her pleas of innocence. 'Obviously you're going to think what you want to think...'

Duarte strode forward and reached for her arms to hold her still when she would have spun away. '*Meu Deus!* What I *want* to think? Do you honestly believe that any man wants to think of his wife in another man's bed?' he raked down at her with charged incredulity, his lean, powerful hands biting into her elbows before he thrust her back from him.

Rage and aggression. That's what she was seeing. Two traits that Emily had once believed that her immensely wealthy, cool and sophisticated husband did not possess. Was he not one of the legendary *baroes*, a baron of Portuguese industry? Not just a banker alone. Duarte had interests in biotechnology, textiles, timber and cork, not to mention ownership of a world famous vineyard that produced wine to die for. One of the old money elite, it was true, but also innovative, tenacious and ruthless as all hell let out. Not a male with a problem in the realm of self-control.

Duarte thrust splayed brown fingers through his luxuriant black hair and breathed in slow and deep. His stunning eyes were veiled by spiky black lashes almost long enough to hit his superb cheekbones which were now scored with faint colour. 'If I frightened you, I'm sorry. It is difficult for me even to look at you in this room.'

Her face flamed and she studied the exquisite handmade pastel rug that adorned the polished floor. The night of that dreadfully boring dinner party she had walked out through the French windows on to the terrace with Toby to enjoy the breeze. How could she have forgotten that location? It did not suggest that she was the world's most sensitive person. *He* remembered—of course he did. But then she had greater cause to want to forget. Her strained eyes burned with tears and she mumbled, 'What can I say?'

'Nothing. The more you say the angrier I become. It is like a chain reaction.'

She couldn't look at him but there was no escape from her own despairing regret. One brief moment in time, one failure to react as her husband had naturally expected her to react with instantaneous rejection, a fatal hesitation that had cost her everything she had, everything she valued. And what a terrible truth it was that people never really appreciated what they *had* until it was taken away without any hope of return, Emily acknowledged painfully.

'I must speak to Victorine. She deserves greater consideration than I granted her on our arrival,' Duarte drawled with a grim lack of intonation. 'I lashed out at her then because I could not defend you against the charge of being what she calls a trollop.'

'You called me a whore...' Emily squeezed out the word from between compressed lips and swallowed hard.

'If I apologised, I'm afraid it would not be with sincerity,' Duarte admitted and the door thudded shut on his departure.

Emily snatched in an uneven breath. Sharing the same house with Duarte promised to be a nightmare, no matter how big the *quinta* was and no matter how infrequent their meetings. He despised her. He was never ever likely to believe that she had not been intimate with Toby. Indeed, Duarte could hardly stand to be in the same room with her. Yet he had kissed her on the flight—well, not at all the way he used to kiss her, she conceded wretchedly. There had been a dark, almost derisive lack of tenderness in that brief encounter and a cold calculated passion she'd never felt in him before. He'd sought out her weakness and exploited it without pity. Duarte had a streak of cruelty she'd never dreamt he possessed.

The housekeeper came to invite Emily to inspect Jamie's nursery. She went upstairs to find a whole bunch of admiring female staff gathered round a beautifully carved wooden cot in the centre of an airy room. Wearing an unfamiliar white sleepsuit, Jamie lay in his crisp blue and yellow bedding and continued to sleep like a log. Emily remained in the doorway, taking in surroundings in which she herself had had no input. Colourful ducks marched round the wallpaper border and bright curtains hung at the windows. The surface of every piece of nursery furniture was packed with waiting toys, many still in their packaging.

Her throat thickened as she appreciated that the room had been prepared long before Duarte had even found his son. Had he bought those toys himself? Gone into a shop, selected them in an act of positive thinking, determined to believe that he would eventually find them and get to bring his child home? Guilt ate her alive and she turned away shame-faced from the sight.

'It's a lovely nursery,' she said in careful Portuguese and she managed an appreciative smile.

The housekeeper led her further down the corridor and spread open the door of a large and beautifully furnished bedroom. Recognising the clothing being carefully put away by a maid as her own, Emily realised that she was now being shown her new quarters. On the other side of the *quinta* from the vast interconnecting bedroom suite she had once shared with Duarte. Just about as far as he could exile her and still keep her within the same walls—but at least she would be close to Jamie, she reminded herself, striving to keep up spirits sagging low enough now to hit the level of the wine cellars.

No sooner had the maid departed than a knock sounded on the door. Hurriedly composing herself, Emily opened the door to find herself facing a uniformed nanny, eager to proclaim her many childcare qualifications, her ability to speak English as fluently as she spoke Portuguese and her family's history of devoted service to the Monteiro family. Emily smiled and nodded repeatedly for not much else seemed to be required from her but she was taken aback and dismayed that Duarte should already have engaged a nanny for their son.

Jamie already had the entire household staff hanging over him like he was the seventh wonder of the world. But then, Duarte himself had been the last infant in the *quinta* nurseries and the Portuguese adored children—her son's arrival was a major event. But Emily felt that the immediate hire of a nanny when she herself had now nothing to do *other* than look after their son was a clear demonstration that Duarte did not consider her responsible enough for the task. Using the internal phone by the bed, she requested her evening meal in her room. She might as well get used to staying out of Duarte's way. He didn't want to see her, speak to her, have anything to do with her—and, in the mood she was in, she did not feel she could even blame him.

It was not as if she had *ever* had any actual proof that Duarte had slept with other women when he was away on business. But he had not come to her bed again after her pregnancy had been confirmed. After a while, pride had demanded that she lock that connecting door between their bedrooms and let him think that she wasn't one bit bothered by his lack of interest.

He was the man who had once murmured to her in the dark of the night and in the oddest tone of self-discovery, 'I have to confess that sex is very important to me.'

The man who had stood straight and tall and said, the day after his marriage proposal had been joyously accepted, 'I'm not in love with you and it is only fair that I should be frank on that score.'

Even after almost two years, the pain of hearing that admission spoken out loud still hurt her. She hadn't wanted him to pretend but she hadn't wanted him to speak those words either. Knowing in her heart of hearts had been one thing, a stark confession almost too much for her to bear. She had adored him and *still* adored him but she'd been so miserable in their marriage that now she could no longer see any point in their continuing such a charade. Just for Jamie's sake? Jamie, the precious child whose father had broken her heart.

When her evening meal arrived on a tray, she ate with no great appetite. Then she freshened up in the en suite bathroom and unravelled her hair from its constraining plait to brush out the tangles. She searched her reflection in the mirror. Emily Monteiro, unwanted, unloved wife. Major failure in the wife stakes, she added fairly. And on *his* terms he had given so much. The wedding ring, the name, the wealth, the security. So what if he had never ever returned her phone calls? So what if he had muttered Izabel's name on several occasions while he slept by her side? So what if he had got bored with her skinny, flat-chested body and engaged in a little discreet infidelity with more exciting and beautiful women?

Well, actually, she registered in the midst of her growing turmoil, Duarte Avila de Monteiro might still be the love of her life but she had pretty much hated him as much as

she loved him once it became clear that her pregnancy concluded his interest in her. Once he had impregnated her,
that had been that. Duty done, mission accomplished. She
closed her aching eyes. The low-maintenance wife project
had gone belly-up when he least expected it.

Sick and tired of her own emotionalism, Emily headed
for the nursery. Jamie was sure to be close to waking and
hungry by now. The door stood ajar and, hearing Duarte
laugh, Emily hesitated in surprise. Then she heard the
nanny issuing serious advice on how best to hold a baby
and just had to sneak a look. She saw Duarte sprawled in
a chair, long powerful legs extended as he held Jamie cra-
dled in his arms and struggled to coordinate a feeding bottle
held at an awkward angle.

'I need another hand,' he groaned in Portuguese.

Yet his lean, boldly masculine profile was relaxed. There
was even the hint of a rueful smile at the corner of his
expressive mouth as he dealt with the unusual experience
of not being an immediate brilliant success at something.
Evidently, he did not mind the young nanny as an audience
to his efforts to get acquainted with his baby son. But he
would not have turned to Emily for similar advice and support. Cut to the bone by that humiliating awareness, Emily
crept back to her room, feeling like the most hated woman
in the world. Even Jamie wasn't crying for her, she reflected painfully.

An hour later when she dared to emerge from her room
again, Jamie was sound asleep in his cot. Emily was dying
to lift her son and hold him close but there was a baby
listener beside the night light. If Jamie cried, the staff would
come running and she would look like an irresponsible
mother. That warning image sent her into retreat.

She was leaving the nursery when Victorine intercepted
her.

'You have Duarte's son. You must be feeling very

pleased with yourself,' the older woman condemned bitterly.

'Please don't feel you have to leave. This is your home,' Emily pointed out, ignoring that opening sally.

The older woman pursed her lips. 'It hasn't been *my* home since you first came into it. When Duarte put someone like you in my daughter's place, he…'

At the sound of that all-too-familiar refrain, Emily suppressed a groan. Once the centre of her mother's world, the late Izabel had been a renowned beauty as famed for her style as her effervescent charm. Unable to come to terms with Izabel's premature death, Victorine had deeply resented Duarte's remarriage.

As the older woman paused for breath in what had grown into a rant freely interspersed with spiteful comparisons, Emily simply sighed, 'Your daughter is no longer here but you're still part of Duarte's family and he's fond of you.'

Frustrated by Emily's lack of reaction to her gibes, Victorine dealt her a look of boiling resentment and hurried back the way she had come. Sticks and stones can break my bones but words can never hurt me, Emily rhymed to herself. But, feeling in dire need of some fresh air, she went out to the charming courtyard at the back of the *quinta*. There she sat on a stone bench in rueful appreciation of the superb box-hedged herbal gardens designed by her talented predecessor. The light was fading fast and using the same service staircase she had employed earlier, she returned to her room to have a shower before bed.

She'd already shed her top and skirt when someone turned the handle on her bedroom door and partially opened it. Freezing in dismay, she heard Duarte's deep drawl as he addressed one of the staff in the corridor and she dived into the bathroom in a panic to snatch up a towel.

'Emily?' Duarte breathed, a raw edge to his dark, rich voice that sent a current of foreboding through her.

She emerged with pronounced reluctance from the bathroom. 'Yes?'

Shimmering golden eyes raked over her shrinking figure and the death grip she had on a towel that was just a little too small for its purpose. She had one unpremeditated clash with his smouldering gaze and she hastily looked away again, her heart jumping as if she had jammed a finger in a live electric socket. The anger she had seen in him earlier was no longer contained. It leapt out at her like a physical entity and radiated around him like a dangerous aura. From the fierce set of his lean dark devastating face, the rigidity of his broad muscular shoulders and the clenching of his long brown fingers into fists, she read a level of unholy rage she'd truly never ever expected to see in a male as self-disciplined as he was.

'How *could* you?' he demanded wrathfully.

'How could I...wh-what?' she stammered, tummy churning at the terrible tension in the atmosphere.

'Don't play games with me unless you want to get hurt...' Duarte ground out. 'Victorine came to me in great distress to tell me how you had taunted her with her daughter's death...'

Emily's knees were locked together and her legs gave an involuntary wobble, the high-heeled mules she still wore providing a far from stable support. 'I didn't taunt her. All I said was that her daughter was no longer here—'

'I don't believe you. It's a very long time since I've seen Izabel's mother in such a state and you cannot even look me in the face.'

Emily could feel herself beginning to *feel* guilty even though she knew that she had said nothing that could have upset the older woman. Nor could she help but recall how enraged Victorine had looked when she'd realised that Emily was no longer a soft target on which to vent her spleen. She lifted her chin, raising strained aquamarine eyes to meet a gaze as stormy as the threatening glow inside a volcano about to erupt. 'She can only have misunderstood what I said—'

'Don't push me on this. Shock is written all over you. Shock that Victorine told tales and your unpleasantness has been exposed for me to deal with—'

'I did not taunt her with Izabel's death. Why would I do that, for goodness' sake?' Emily prompted on a rising note of protest.

'Because, as the mother of my son and my wife, you might well feel that you have a great deal of power in this house.'

A nervous giggle bubbled up out of Emily's constricted throat. 'Power? *Me?* I was less important than the most junior housemaid the last time I lived here! Victorine was always picking out my mistakes in front of the staff, embarrassing them, humiliating me...' As Emily's voice ebbed in recollection, it then gathered renewed steam. 'Nothing I ever did pleased her *or* you. I spent hours trying to make up menus, only to have them rejected. I got to the stage where I didn't care if you never ate again! I let her march me out to the endless coffee mornings, the polite social visits, the charity functions, the dinner parties for which you never turned up and I changed my clothes at least four times a flippin' day—'

'Emily,' Duarte gritted.

'Do you know something?' Emily proclaimed with the fierce bitterness that assailed her when she recalled how desperately hard she had worked to fill her role as a high society wife. 'I'd have had an easier ride down a nineteenth-century coal mine than I had being your wife!'

That last phrase dropped into a silence so deep that a feather could have fallen and sounded out a resounding crash. Duarte surveyed her with hard dark eyes. 'You condemn yourself with every word you say. It's obvious that

you've *always* resented Victorine's presence here and
would very much prefer to see her move out.'

Emily's lips opened and then very slowly closed again,
her eyes widening in dismay as she realised what Duarte
had extracted from her unfortunate outburst. Suddenly she
could have bitten out her own impulsive tongue but innate
honesty prevented her from lying. It was true—no way
could she put her hand on her heart and say that she had
not resented his mother-in-law in the past. Regimented by
Victorine into a lifestyle she loathed and then continually
criticised and shown up in front of others as she failed to
fill the hallowed shoes of her superhuman predecessor,
Emily had often wished that Victorine would magically
vanish from her horizon.

'But it wasn't like that tonight, Duarte,' she argued ve-
hemently. 'I *know* you're fond of her and I reminded her
of that and asked her to think again—'

'I have more trust in her ability to tell the truth than I
have in yours. If you ever do anything like this again, you
will pay a high price. *Don't* turn away from me like that!'
Duarte raked at her, making her flinch.

So now as well as being the most hated person in the
house and a trollop and that other word which she could
bear to recall even less, she was also a nasty shrew and an
outright liar. Emily kept on turning away, for she had too
much pride to let him see how savaged she was by his
refusal to place even the smallest trust in her word.

Long powerful fingers settled on her slight shoulder and
flipped her back again with a masculine strength that was
far from reassuring. 'When I say jump, now you say, "How
high?" Haven't you got that message yet?'

'No...and I won't,' Emily told him, her gaze glimmering
with angry tears. 'You are not going to make me feel any
worse about myself than I already feel!'

'So *you* feel bad?' Duarte loosed a derisive laugh that

broke the surging tension with the disturbing effect of shattering glass. 'But I bet not one tenth as bad as *I* felt about bringing you back into my home this evening...'

Emily dropped her head and tried to swallow the great fat lump of guilt in her throat. She was in turmoil, wanting to scream and sob and attack him all at one and the same time. Once again she'd been her own worst enemy. Why, oh why had she been foolish enough to even *speak* to Victorine? Why hadn't she just minded her own wretched business and walked away? But she knew why, didn't she? She had not wanted to feel that the older woman's departure was yet one more sin to be piled up at her door.

'But now you're about to make me feel much better about that difficult decision,' Duarte completed in a charged undertone that sent the oddest tremor down her responsive spine.

'Oh...and how am I going to do that?' she prompted chokily, fighting to hold the tears back until he left her again. He hated her, he absolutely hated her and she could not imagine how she had ever managed to persuade herself that Duarte had no truly strong emotions where she was concerned.

'Sex.'

Engaged in an apparently enraptured scrutiny of his soft leather loafers, Emily blinked rapidly in receipt of that explanation. Mentally she strained to persuade herself that he had not uttered that single unexpected word with the smooth cool of a male who had already overcome his anger while she was still struggling even to *think* like a rational being.

The silence seemed to rush and eddy around her like a high wind.

She raised her gaze to the well-cut beige chinos sheathing his long, long powerful length of leg and lean hips, up more slowly still to the belt encircling his narrow waist and the casual white shirt open at his bronzed throat.

'Sex...?' Emily almost whispered as if it physically hurt her to say the word.

Duarte lifted a lean hand and pushed up her chin. Volatile golden eyes set between spiky black lashes inspected her disbelieving face. *'Sim, querida.'*

Yes, he said in confirmation but her brain refused to credit the evidence of her hearing.

CHAPTER FIVE

'S-sex?' Emily stammered helplessly.

'The concept appeals and intrigues,' Duarte murmured silkily.

Emily drew in a very ragged breath but still her voice was faint. 'Does it really? Tell me, when did this sudden attack of lust occur to you? Is this like…your equivalent of that ancestor of yours who bricked his wife up alive in a wall?'

'Such a very insightful question, *querida*.' Duarte surveyed her with brilliant dark eyes alight with hard amusement. 'But rather naive. I don't need to explain myself to you and why would I?'

As Duarte narrowed the distance between them, Emily went as rigid as a porcupine going on the offensive. 'Don't you dare touch me!'

Duarte scanned the flushed oval of her delicate face, his strong jawline hardening. 'Perhaps I want to remind you that you're mine. Perhaps it *is* that basic…I don't care.'

'Basic's not me,' Emily framed unevenly because she trusted herself even less than she trusted him. She could feel his proximity with every skin cell she possessed. In her mind's eye she could even visualise every shameless skin cell sitting up and begging and that made her cringe. For what had always lain at the very heart of Duarte's total irresistibility had been the simple truth that her *own* resistance was nil.

He hooked a lean brown finger into the towel she was still clutching. 'Overkill, don't you think?'

She trembled, a liquid sensation of heat pooling deep

inside her, her legs welding her to the spot. He was so close she could smell the warm male scent of his sunwarmed skin, so close she could feel deliciously threatened by the sheer size differential between her and the potent masculinity of his lean hard physique.

'You signed up for your own personal punishment plan while we were still airborne,' Duarte delivered in a tone as smooth as silk.

She was staring up at him, wholly enveloped in her own growing reaction to him. It had always been that way, which was why when things were wrong between them she just never looked directly at him, out of fear that he would guess how great his power was. Only now, she'd reached the point where she could not stop staring, drinking in every taut angle of that strikingly dark and handsome face of his, the proud arrogant jut of his nose, the fabulous cheekbones that lent his features such pronounced strength and definition, the fine grain of his skin that roughened round his hard jawline. And still she was not satisfied; still it was not enough to satiate that need within her.

'S-sorry? Punishment plan?' she echoed a whole ten seconds after he had finished speaking and only after frantically plundering her memory.

'My kind of punishment,' Duarte spelt out with measured satisfaction.

Stunning dark golden eyes held hers as he finally jerked loose the screening towel so that it drifted down into a heap on the rug. Strong hands lifted to snap round her wrists and prevent her startled attempt to stoop and retrieve it.

'Duarte...?' Emily gasped, very much taken back by his behaviour.

He held her back from him and let his intent gaze roam at a leisurely pace over her slim, slight figure. She tried to curve away from him, curl in protectively on herself while still standing, but he held fast to her. Visually exploring the rise and fall of her small breasts beneath the barrier of her bra, his attention strolled down to her tiny waist and the swell of her hips where a pair of white cotton panties that were not of the diminutive variety shut off his view.

'The cotton look was fine when sweet and wholesome was the draw but it's not to my taste now,' Duarte confided while Emily's pale skin coloured up like the rising sun beneath an appraisal that was reducing her to agonies of embarrassment. 'And since pleasing me must necessarily *be* your top priority—'

'*Why*? Why would it be?' she broke in, wild in her humiliation.

'Security of tenure,' Duarte specified in cool warning. 'And please let's ditch the I'm-so-shy routine I used to respect because I don't respect it any more.'

Her heart was thudding so fast, she could hardly catch her breath. 'It wasn't a routine—'

'But it must have been,' Duarte asserted in interruption as he backed her inexorably in the direction of the bed. 'All those hot afternoons you spent in *his* studio in pursuit of a surprise portrait supposedly for me? At a time when you had locked the door between our bedrooms you were attending all those sittings purely for my benefit? And you're *still* trying to persuade me that the same lout that I personally heard swearing eternal devotion to you never laid a finger on you?'

Emily nodded jerkily, conscious of how very unlikely he made her being innocent sound but still ready to argue. 'I was hardly ever alone with him. He had a girlfriend—'

Duarte elevated a winged dark brow. 'Get a better story. Or even better, tell me exactly what you *did* do with him—'

As he swept her up into his arms and settled her squarely down on the centre of the big bed and stepped back from her, she said feverishly. 'Nothing, absolutely nothing.'

'I beat the hell out of him,' Duarte informed her with chilling exactitude.

Suddenly the atmosphere was sizzling like a stick of dynamite ready to blow. In considerable shock, Emily gazed back at Duarte, all her colour ebbing—for the very last thing she would have expected from Duarte was that kind of violence.

'That was my right,' Duarte stated soft and low and dark, watching her like a hawk ready to pounce, smouldering dark golden eyes welded to her sincerely shaken face. 'Do you think that I didn't know that he followed you to the villa in the Douro? That he repeatedly attempted to see you? And that when that failed, he kept on phoning?'

A pin could have been heard dropping in her appalled silence.

Duarte studied her with a hard force she could feel in every atom of her being. 'If you had encouraged him then, if you had *once* spoken to him or seen him, you would not be here now.'

So throughout that winter she'd passed at the country house, nothing that happened there had gone unreported to Duarte. Emily was genuinely shattered by that discovery. 'We...we were separated,' she whispered shakily.

Savage anger flared in his blazing look of challenge. 'You were still my wife and what is mine stays mine until *I* choose to relinquish it!'

Before her she saw a male with traits she had failed to recognise before. The male that existed behind the deceptive patina of sophistication and cool courtesy. A more primitive breed of male, every bit as aggressive and possessive of what was his as any backstreet fighter. She'd never been so shaken in her whole life—for only then it occurred to her that naturally, Duarte used the same forceful drives for his personal life that he used every day in a more civilised way in business—in that field his ruthlessness was a living legend.

'Turning him away in the Douro was the only thing you did right,' Duarte pronounced grittily.

Emily was now realising that the only reason that Duarte had left her alone on the bed was to undress. She lay there with the curious sensation of being weighted to the mattress while she watched him finish unbuttoning his shirt. As he bent to remove his shoes, the shirt hung loose, disclosing an enervating glimpse of a broad chest the colour of living bronze, with dark curling hair emphasising his powerful pectoral muscles and the hard flat contours of his stomach. Her breath locked in her throat. As he straightened to his full six foot four inches, she couldn't take her eyes from him. He was a stunning vision of raw masculinity and it had been so long since she had seen him like that. Indeed, it was over a year since they had shared the smallest intimacy, she reminded herself, dimly seeking excuse for her total absorption in him.

'There will be no separate bedrooms this time, *no* locked doors,' Duarte spelt out, sending the zip rasping down on his chinos, angling his narrow hips in a slight movement that she found inexplicably but hugely sexy.

Her fair skin coloured up hotly on that straying thought and, dredging her eyes from him in severe embarrassment, she focused on the edge of the linen sheet already neatly folded down by a maid in readiness for an occupant. *Two* occupants, she reflected, her brain moving at a tenth of its usual capacity. Duarte was going to make love to her. It occurred to her that saying 'no' was still an option and that she really ought to say something.

'I really don't want this,' Emily told him.

'Just who are you trying to kid?'

Aghast at that blunt comeback, Emily blinked in dismay and was betrayed into a sudden upward glance. Duarte sur veyed her in flagrant challenge, sardonic amusement gleaming at her shaken expression. He stood there naked and magnificent, his hard shaft fully erect.

'You are not chained to the bed but you're not running anywhere. Why?'

For a timeless moment, she simply stared at him, seriously wrongfooted by that enquiry. Throwing her a look of irredeemably male logic, Duarte came down on the bed and reached for her so fast, she gave a stifled gasp of fright.

'Let me tell you *why*,' he urged, knotting long fingers into her tumbled red-gold hair as he brought her up against his hard muscular chest. 'I can turn you on just by looking at you!'

Crushed into the unyielding strength of him yet forced to maintain an eye contact that she would have done just about anything to avoid, Emily felt as if she was fighting for her last ounce of pride. 'No...not any more—'

He tugged her head back, shimmering eyes scorching down into hers. 'So what was that little demonstration of total surrender on the jet, then? One last fling?'

Her whole body was already reacting to the steely contours of his with insidious little quivers of heat and a drowning weakness that was even more dangerous to her self-discipline. The fresh warm scent of him was in her nostrils with every breath she drew, achingly familiar, achingly erotic. 'You...you took me by surprise—'

'*Nâo te acredito*... I don't believe you,' Duarte derided, his breath fanning her cheek and then his hot hard hungry mouth claiming hers with a raw assurance that made denial impossible.

It was a shattering kiss, full of explosive demand. His tongue stabbed into the tender moist interior of her mouth and plundered the sweetness with an invasive force that made her heart hammer as fast as if she'd run a three minute mile. She trembled beneath that onslaught, her hands clenching, nails biting into her palms as she attempted to withstand the raw sexual enticement of his expert mouth on hers. But the little kernel of nagging heat he had already awakened low in her belly was too seductive. She started shifting in his grasp, pushing into him in a helpless surge and all the time, Dear heaven, I want him, want him, *want him*, was running like a charged mantra through her mind.

'Indeed, belief would be a great challenge,' Duarte husked, ungenerous in victory as only a rogue male can be—and then he did something that truly shook her. Taking her hand, he curled her fingers round his bold erection. 'That's more like it...'

He felt like hot steel sheathed in silk. Her hand shook a little and her face burned scarlet at being asked to do what she had previously only done in darkness and beneath concealing covers. But an undeniable excitement gripped her and she stroked his hard masculinity, feeling the inexorable surge of answering heat between her trembling thighs.

In response, he caught her back to him and mated his mouth to hers with ferocious hunger. Then he drew back from her when she was clinging to him. Her hands dropped from him and she was disorientated by the sensation of her breasts coming free from her bra without her having had anything to do with it. She glanced down at herself to see that the front fastening had already been undone. Even as she whipped up her hands to cover herself, Duarte was ahead of her, imprisoning her fingers in his own, forestalling her.

'Stop it...' she gasped, embarrassed by the sight of her own bare flesh because she felt that she could not compare to other women with the small pouting swells crowned by rosy distended nipples.

Duarte used his superior strength to flatten her back on to the bed and stared down at her with hot hungry eyes of appreciation. 'You can't hide the evidence of your own desire,' he breathed, lowering his head to capture a swollen, throbbing tip between his lips.

Her entire body jerked, for she had always been almost unbearably sensitive there. Her hands flexed within the hold of his and he released them but she dug her fingers into the sheets beneath her instead. Excitement was like a damburst inside her, pressure building up with every second and she could not withstand her own intense need to be touched. A low keening sound was torn from her as he tormented the rosy crests with the kind of skill that drove her absolutely wild. So somehow they got to the stage where he was holding her down purely to keep her still and her hands had, seemingly without an input from her, risen to lace into his luxuriant black hair, urging him on in helpless writhing yearning.

'So tell me you're not mine now, *minha pequena esposa*,' Duarte invited, a roughened edge to his dark, deep drawl as he lifted his head from the glistening buds still begging for his attention.

'Don't stop...*please*,' she heard herself beg like a supplicant and even as she said it she knew she would cringe for herself later, but just then the sheer craving he had unleashed took precedence.

'Was it like this with Jarrett?'

For a split second she could not think who 'Jarrett' was. Toby, Bliss's cousin. Toby Jarrett. The name stood out in her mind's eye and made her tummy clench. She gazed up at Duarte, suddenly as terrified as an animal knowing it was about to be slaughtered, and knowing that there was absolutely nothing she could do about it because he wouldn't believe her.

'You are just sick with shame,' Duarte bit out, studying her as if he had her under a microscope and could read every nuance of expression.

She shut her eyes on the hot scorch of threatening tears.

Even while her wretched body leapt and burned for him and her every thought was at bay, *he* was still in sufficient control to attack.

'Much good that does either of us,' Duarte growled in an oddly ragged undertone and then suddenly he was gathering her back into his arms, reclaiming her mouth with a kind of blazing fiery desire that went through her quivering body like sheet lightning. He shuddered against her and then he stilled and, for a split second of horror, she thought he was about to pull free of her and instinctively she wrapped her arms round him as tightly as she could.

And then she felt a long forefinger stroking her cheek where a tear had escaped and left a telling trail and he cursed in Portuguese. He claimed her lips again at the same time as his exploring hand teased the aching points of her breasts. That instant of all too painful self-awareness was sent into oblivion by the renewed force of her own response.

'Duarte…' she moaned at the peak of an almost agonised gasp as his stroking fingers discovered the dampness of the triangle of fabric stretched taut between her restive thighs.

He stripped away that last barrier and found the hot moist core of her femininity. Her heartbeat seemed to thunder in her own ears as her body writhed without her volition. There was only wild sensation and overwhelming hunger for anything that would ease the tormenting ache of pressure clawing at her. She could feel him against her thigh, hot and hard and rampantly aroused and just knowing that she could still have that effect on him intensified everything that she felt.

'I can't be gentle…' he groaned, rising over her and parting her thighs with impatient hands to haul her back to him.

'Doesn't matter…'

Nothing mattered then but the driving thrust with which he entered her. Her body was just one gigantic source of longing and then he was there, dominantly male, stretching her with his strength and fullness and there was so much intense pleasure she cried out against it.

'Emily, *meu bonita…*'

My beautiful one, she savoured in stunned surprise and gazed up at him to register the hard-edged need etched into his lean dark devastating face but saw the concern in his hot golden eyes. 'I hurt you?' he prompted.

She shook her head, beyond speech, and even if she could have spoken she could not have thought of any way to tell him that that much pleasure came close to pain. But it seemed he understood, for a flash of raw male amusement flared in his spectacular eyes and he came into her again, hard and fast and not to be denied. She arched her hips up to him in helpless encouragement. He set a raw sensual rhythm that heightened her excitement to a level she could not control. There was nothing but him and the wild surging rise of her own excitement, her own primal delight in his erotic dominance. Every pulse racing, his name on her lips, she reached the dazzling instant of release and cried out in ecstasy at the explosive charge of sensation pulsating through her in waves. She clung to him as he shuddered over her and vented a ragged groan of intense satisfaction.

Happiness was bubbling up inside her now. To be so close to Duarte again, to feel so at home, to feel needed, wanted, *secure*. As he freed her of his weight, she followed him across the bed to stay close. She buried her face in a smooth brown muscular shoulder and drank in the hot, husky scent of him like an addict. One arm sliding round his neck, she lay across him, happy but engaged in frantic thought. Intimacy was the foundation stone of any normal marriage. My goodness, what had possessed her when she had briefly believed that she ought to be saying no?

In fact, so strong was her sense of joy and relief that she

had not made that foolish mistake, she found herself muttering feverishly, 'You're just so fantastic...'

Part of her cringed for herself even as she said it and then she noticed how rigid he was under her and how silent. Not that in the aftermath, Duarte had ever been exactly chatty. But she also became agonisingly aware that he did not have his arms round her and that she was the one making all the effort to be cosy and close and warmly intimate. About then, she just started wanting to die.

'And you're so affectionate, *querida*,' Duarte breathed a little stiltedly and then he finally curved an arm round her slim, still length and smoothed warm fingers down her taut spinal cord.

'Stop it...' she whispered.

'Stop what?'

'I can feel you thinking,' she mumbled, sensing his mental distance from her with every atom of ESP she possessed.

'I am thinking that I need a shower,' Duarte said drily.

And why was he thinking that? A shower would get him back out of bed again, away from *her*, she reflected miserably, a mass of insecurities unleashed inside her again. But he couldn't stay in the shower forever, could he? Slowly she edged away from him again, hoping to be snatched back; it didn't happen. He rolled lithely over and sprang out of bed. All potent male, hair-roughened skin and rippling muscles. Absolutely gorgeous but never hers, never really hers even at the beginning and even less likely to be now after what had happened eleven months ago.

Emily pulled herself up against the tumbled pillows, reading the raw tension in his wide shoulders but unable to silence her own desperate need to be heard. 'Duarte?'

'What?' he growled like a grizzly bear.

He was *so* volatile, she registered in amazement. How had she never seen that in him before? Had she been so wrapped up in her own self-pity that she'd never appreciated that she was married to a male who literally seemed to boil beneath the surface of that cool front with dark, deep, dangerous emotion?

'I've got to say it…I'm sorry,' she muttered feverishly, plucking nervously at the corner of the sheet beneath her hand. 'No matter how bad it looked, I never felt anything for Toby and I never had an affair with him either—'

Duarte swung back to her with the speed of a lion ready to spring. Angry golden eyes struck sparks off hers in a look as physical as a slap on the face. 'Don't you know when to keep quiet?'

Shrinking back into the pillows and pale as death, Emily whispered, 'I *need* you to listen—'

Duarte threw up both hands in a violent gesture of lost patience and strode on into the bathroom.

She listened to the shower coming on full gush and a sense of defeat engulfed her. It was swiftly followed by the conviction that she was the most stupid woman in existence. Why was she always so naive with him? *Sex*, he had said before she succumbed to her dream of how she wanted it to be. And so lost had she got in that delusion that, in the aftermath of passion, she had swarmed all over him as if nothing had ever been wrong between them, but it had been only sex as far as he was concerned, not making love, not a meeting of minds. Incredibly exciting sex, in her opinion, but then what did she really know about what it was like for *him*?

Just the slaking of a physical hunger on the nearest most available female body? Well, she'd certainly made herself available. Exactly as he had expected. *I can turn you on just by looking at you.* She stuffed her hot face into the cooling linen. Her own personal punishment plan, he had said—and what had he meant by that? And why hadn't she asked? Her sated body told her where her mind had been. Lost. Wanting him, wanting him much more than common sense. She'd had no restraint. She had so desperately wanted to believe that physical intimacy could fill the terrible emptiness that losing him had filled her with, could provide the first bridge between them, could give her back *hope*. Her nails raked down the smooth sheet beneath the pillows, self-hatred burning her like poison.

Suddenly, she pulled herself up and back on her knees, thrusting her wildly tangled hair back over her shoulders. Her strained face taut, she leapt off the bed, looked around for something to pull on to hide her nakedness and snatched up his discarded shirt. She came to a halt on the threshold of the bathroom where Duarte was already towelling himself dry.

'I suppose you think everything you ever thought about me has been proven now…I suppose you think I *am* a whore!' she fired at him jaggedly.

Duarte raked a driven hand through his damp tousled hair and rested dark deepset brooding eyes on her in the tension-filled silence. 'Leave it,' he warned and tossing the towel aside, he strode past her.

Her legs felt horribly wobbly. She leant back against the bedroom wall to steady herself. A tight hard knot of pain was building inside her, threatening to take control of her entirely, no matter how hard she tried to get a grip on herself. 'Sleeping with me was like a power play, was it?' she mumbled sickly. 'A case of finding out how high you could make me jump? And just how desperate I would be to please you?'

'I told you to *leave* it…' Duarte ground out, the long sweep of his muscular golden back rigid with stormy tension as he hauled on his chinos.

Emily felt she'd already been reduced so low that nothing else could hurt her. However, it belatedly dawned on her that he was getting dressed again and that he wasn't staying the rest of the night and that seemed the lowest blow of all. 'Where are you going?'

Duarte swung back round to face her, his lean strong features ferociously set. 'Any place I don't have to listen to you getting it all wrong—'

'How am I getting it wrong?' she pressed in desperation. 'Duarte?'

Brilliant eyes grim, he let a harsh laugh escape. 'Do you think this is so easy for me? I'm thinking about you with Jarrett almost all the time. I can't get it out of my head...'

Her tummy twisted, her drawn face tightening.

'So all kudos to me for pulling off a fantastic performance between the sheets.' His derision, whether angled at her or himself made her flinch. 'Two years ago, I was your first lover and that meant something to me. Now it's all gone and I am just so bloody angry with you that I don't know why I brought you back here!'

She felt dead inside because he had killed her hopes. She was being rejected again. 'It was only a kiss and I didn't even like it...' she framed strickenly.

'If you open the subject one more time... Where the hell is my shirt?' he demanded in raw completion.

Realising that he had yet to notice what she was wearing, she peeled off his shirt and threw it back at his feet.

Duarte stared at her with pronounced intensity. She stood there like a statue, her hair falling round her like tongues of fire against her fair skin but for once she made no move to cover herself.

'Take your blasted shirt and get out!' she suddenly gasped.

He flicked it up, the movement all grace and derision somehow perfectly combined. She yanked open the door, spread it wide.

Duarte threw her a sardonic look. 'If you were looking

for a guy who turns the other cheek, you shouldn't have married a Monteiro.'

She slammed the door shut on his exit, turned the key in the lock and then ran all the way back to the bed to throw herself facedown on the mattress.

Almost simultaneously it seemed the noise of a sudden jarring crash sent her rolling over in shock to glance back in the direction of the door. She was just in time to see it smash back against the wall. She focused on Duarte, who had kicked it open, with shaken eyes of disbelief. He stood there with clenched fists, breathing heavily, all powerful and quite unashamed masculinity.

'You lock a door against me again and I'll break it down every time!' Outraged golden eyes assailed hers with pure aggressive force. 'Do you understand?'

Very slowly and carefully, she nodded.

CHAPTER SIX

HAVING scarcely slept during a night of emotional turmoil, Emily was up early the following morning and in the nursery with Jamie.

When his nanny found her there, the young woman smiled in understanding and left them in peace. Given lots of cuddles, Jamie was in the sunniest of moods, but soon his big brown eyes turned sleepy again. His every need met, Jamie had an enviable capacity to be as happy in Portugal as he had been in England.

Emily had a shower and put on a denim skirt and tee-shirt. A maid brought her breakfast and she had it out on the balcony—white coffee and wonderful fresh-baked bread served with home-made honey. She was told in answer to her enquiry that 'Don Duarte' had left for his Lisbon office shortly before eight.

It promised to be a glorious day. Surrounded by woods of pine, eucalyptus and oak, the gardens were lush and tropical, full of spiky palms and superb flowering shrubs, the extensive lawns already being industriously watered by the gardeners. Beyond the trees stretched the extensive *quinta* estate of orange and lemon and olive groves. Against the backdrop of the purple green mountains, the tiny village houses sprinkled the hillside like toys. In every direction the views were breathtaking.

Emily had missed Portugal so much during her absence yet, two years earlier, she knew she'd severely underestimated the challenges of marrying a male who not only did not love her but also whose world and expectations were so very different from her own...

Even their wedding had not been what she had wanted. Duarte had desired neither frills nor fuss and, as she loved him, she'd suppressed her longing for a wedding gown and worn a suit. Lunch had followed at an exclusive hotel but it had been attended only by her family and a handful of Duarte's business acquaintances.

'I'd call it a bit shabby,' her sister Hermione had said with a sniff. 'Are you *sure* this isn't a shotgun do?'

From the instant she'd told her family that she was marrying Duarte, the humiliating suggestion that he might only be marrying her because she had fallen pregnant had been repeatedly raised. When her denials were received with cynical disbelief, it had done nothing for her self-image.

Duarte had even been too busy for a honeymoon and they had been married for a week before she discovered that she was *not* his first wife. Studying their marriage certificate with dreamy eyes, she'd finally noticed that he was described as a widower.

'Why didn't you tell me?' she had asked in astonished hurt.

'It wasn't relevant,' Duarte had told her flatly.

Pressing for further details, she had naturally been shocked to learn of the car crash that had killed both Izabel and his twin, Elena. But she'd also noticed that that night, for the first time, Duarte didn't make love to her. Early on, she had learnt that trying to talk about Izabel drove Duarte from her. That same evening, sadly, Jazz, the dog she had adored and whom she had credited with bringing her and Duarte together, had passed away in his sleep and that concluded their stay in England.

Duarte had brought her home to the *quinta* and that very first day, Victorine had invited Emily to her private sitting room where there were framed photographs showing her late daughter Izabel, glorious in her fabulous wedding gown, Izabel on her Caribbean honeymoon, Izabel entertaining royalty...Izabel...Izabel...Izabel. Emily had learnt right then that she was a second-best wife.

A knock on the bedroom door forced Emily from her introspection. Victorine was trying not to look at the lock which Duarte had broken the night before. Emily flushed for naturally the older woman would know that she and Duarte had had a row. The whole household would be buzzing with the sheer shock value of Duarte doing something that much out of character.

'May we speak?' Victorine asked stiffly.

Emily was dumbfounded to see tears glistening in the older woman's shadowed eyes.

'I've seen your son. He is a very beautiful baby...' Victorine told her heavily. 'I feel great guilt that I lied about what you said to me last night and I could not sleep. I told Duarte the truth at breakfast.'

That astonishing confession froze Emily to the spot. At the same time, however, she could not help thinking that if what Victorine was telling her was true, Duarte had certainly not hurtled upstairs to offer *her* an apology for misjudging her.

'I am sorry for the way I have treated you,' Victorine continued doggedly. 'When I saw your son, who is the future of this family, I asked myself how much my unkindness might have contributed to your separation from Duarte last year—'

'Never mind, it's over...forgotten,' Emily broke in awkwardly, finally recognising that Victorine had indeed faced the results of her resentment and had emerged much chastened from the experience.

In revealing discomfiture, Victorine looked away from the damaged door. 'I've made trouble between you and Duarte but it won't happen again. The maids are packing for me.'

As Victorine turned away, looking old and frail and forlorn in her unhappiness, Emily touched her thin arm in a sympathetic gesture. 'You don't need to leave for my benefit.'

'Duarte said I must. He is very disappointed in me and very angry—'

'He'll get over that,' Emily asserted as Victorine began to sob, her fragile self-control splintering at the prospect before her. 'So you and I got off to a bad start but I just can't imagine this place without you and where are you going to go anyway?'

'Two years ago, Duarte said to me, ''Emily is so sweet, so kind, you will love her''…and I *hated* you before I even met you!' the older woman wept.

Emily took Victorine back to her own rooms, knowing how much she would dislike any of the staff seeing her in tears. She began to understand that it had been her own change in attitude the night before which had ultimately led to the present situation. Unable to bully Emily as she had once done, Victorine had lied to Duarte and had then been horrified by her own behaviour. It was odd how good could sometimes come out of bad, Emily was thinking as she went downstairs after calming the other woman down.

It seemed to be a day for surprises: Bliss was in the main hall speaking to the *quinta* housekeeper. Clad in a simple navy dress that was a marvellous foil for her blonde beauty, Bliss moved to greet her.

'I had no idea you were here!' Smiling, Emily asked the housekeeper to serve coffee.

'Strictly in a business capacity, I'm afraid, so I can't stay for long.' Bliss sank down gracefully on a silk-upholstered sofa in the salon. 'Duarte has a big party arranged for this weekend. I was just checking the final arrangements. I've been acting as your husband's hostess since your departure.'

Unsettled by that news and quick to pick up on the brittle

quality of her friend's manner, Emily said in surprise. 'Didn't Victorine object?'

'That hateful old cow?' Bliss laughed. 'Oh, not being a softy like you, I soon settled *her*! I let her know that her ideas about entertaining were fifty years out of date and an embarrassment to Duarte. Ever since then, when there are guests, she takes an early night.'

That unfeeling explanation filled Emily with uneasy distaste. Victorine had her flaws but Emily would never have dreamt of referring to the older woman in such terms. 'Bliss—'

Bliss merely talked over her. 'Mind you, I never thought I'd see *you* back here again either. I was very annoyed when you did your vanishing act last year.'

Grateful for that honesty, Emily spoke up immediately. 'I'm really sorry I didn't keep in touch but—'

'That's not what I'm talking about. When I told you about that little chat I overheard between your husband and his lawyer, I was warning you to get your own legal advice instead of sitting on the fence, hoping all that nasty divorce stuff would go away. I wasn't expecting you to flee the country and put everybody into a loop trying to find you!'

Emily paled at that censorious clarification.

'In tipping you off, I felt like I had *personally* deprived Duarte of his child,' Bliss admitted in no more comforting continuance. 'What on earth possessed you? And now to come back here, regardless of how Duarte feels about you—'

'What are you saying?' Emily faltered in growing shock at what she was hearing.

'Come on, Emily…all Duarte cared about was getting his son back and resident in Portugal. Now he's got him, he won't let you take him away again. In a marriage that was failing from day one, where does that leave you?'

'I've never discussed Duarte or our relationship with you,' Emily reminded the other woman uncomfortably.

Her exquisite face an icy mask, Bliss rose to her feet. 'Well, excuse me for presuming on our former friendship—'

Emily flew upright in distress. 'No, Bliss...I didn't *mean*—'

'Don't come crying to me when you find yourself divorced and without your precious son!' Bliss told her scornfully. 'Can't you see the bigger picture here? Doesn't it occur to you that Duarte may already have another woman in his life?'

Emily's tummy gave a sick somersault and she could barely credit that the blonde was a woman she had once believed was a true friend. 'Why are you behaving like this?'

'Maybe you should have settled for my cousin, Toby, while you had the chance,' Bliss derided dulcetly before she departed, leaving Emily standing in the salon in a stricken daze.

Had Duarte met someone else? Well, why not, a little voice demanded. Wouldn't he have felt he had every excuse to find solace elsewhere? She could feel herself inwardly coming apart at the seams under the new stress which Bliss had imposed on her already overwrought system.

She'd just heard Bliss's car driving off when a phone was brought to her.

It was Duarte on the line. 'Will you meet me for lunch?'

Emily blinked in disconcertion. Duarte was neither in the habit of phoning her during his working day nor of inviting her to meet him for lunch.

'I have something to tell you,' he murmured tautly.

A woman who drove him to smashing locked doors open was *not* for him. He regretted bringing her back to Portugal, recognised his mistake. No, more probably he planned to tell her that he had met someone else. Slow, agonised tears started trekking down her cheeks.

'Emily?' he prompted. 'I'll send a car for you. Please come.'

He rang off without another word. She went upstairs to see if the more dressy clothes which she had left behind when they separated were still intact in the room she had once occupied. They were. She fingered through the many options available. Cerise pink, fire-engine red, fluorescent orange, traffic-stopping purple. Picking the jazzy pink which hurt her aching eyes, she got changed. He was going to dump her again. She *knew* he was. Last night, he had more or less said right out how hard he had had to push himself to go to bed with her again. Mind you, at the time, he'd *seemed* fairly enthusiastic!

The car ferried her the thirty-odd kilometres into Lisbon. Duarte had a superb apartment on the Avenida da Libertade and, as she ascended from the car in the long tree-lined boulevard, sick butterflies were dancing in her tummy.

Ushered into the imposing drawing room where she'd once fallen ingloriously asleep during a supper with his friends, following an evening at the opera, she focused on Duarte. Her heart started behaving as if someone was playing football with it and her mouth ran dry.

Poised by one of the tall nineteenth-century windows, black hair gleaming in the sunlight, his elegant light-grey pinstripe suit cut to fit his broad shoulders and long powerful thighs, Duarte looked absolutely spectacular. Studying those lean, darkly handsome features of his and hurriedly evading those all-seeing, all-knowing, stunning golden eyes, she ran out of breath. Suddenly, all she could think about was the passion of the night hours and all she could feel was the intimate ache that still lingered at the core of her own body as a result.

'Thank you for coming,' Duarte said with grave quietness.

'I'd never have the nerve to stand you up,' Emily confided, her fingers biting so hard into the clutch purse she was holding that her hands were hurting. 'Where are we going for lunch?'

'I thought we could eat here.'

Instantly, she felt trapped. True, a public place was hardly suitable for the delivery of any revelation likely to *upset*. But couldn't he just have waited until he came home for dinner? Instead, she'd been summoned like a schoolgirl to hear her fate and that felt distinctly humiliating.

'Do I have to eat?' she enquired brittlely. 'I'm not hungry.'

'As you wish. Would you like a drink?'

'A brandy...' She glanced at him while he dealt with her request, seeing the tension etched in the hard cast of his bronzed profile. The atmosphere was so strained, she felt an unwary word might snap it in two.

Sitting down on the edge of an opulent antique sofa, she sipped nervously at the brandy.

'This morning, Victorine admitted that she'd deliberately mislead me about what you said to her—'

'I know. She also spoke to me and apologised,' Emily responded.

Duarte paced forward from the window and moved his hands in a very expressive gesture of regret. 'I misjudged you and I owe you a very big apology for I have never known you to be cruel.'

Emily shrugged jerkily, unable to reap the smallest satisfaction from that acknowledgement. 'It was just another metaphoric stick to beat me with, wasn't it?'

Dulled colour rose to accentuate the strong slant of his high cheekbones. 'You may be right. However, when my former mother-in-law then went on to confess that she'd

resented you from the very hour that I married you, I was
very much shocked.'

Surprised though Emily was that Victorine had gone that
far in her need to ease her conscience, Emily simply sighed.
She was more concerned about what he might have to say
next.

'I was foolish to believe that Victorine would easily accept another woman as my wife,' Duarte stated with a
harshened edge to his dark, deep drawl. 'Had I not had a
board meeting early this morning, I would've come to
speak to you immediately.'

'Well, business first and last,' Emily breathed helplessly.
'There's nothing new in that.'

'No…but I think today business came first because it was
easier to handle,' Duarte conceded, startling her with that
frank admission. 'Naturally I feel guilty. Our home should
have been the one place where you could feel relaxed and
content but Victorine's spite must've made you very unhappy.'

Emily felt like a stone. Old resentments and bitterness
had hardened her usually soft heart. 'I always blamed *you*
more than I blamed her…'

Duarte's golden eyes zeroed in on her and narrowed. The
taut set of his jawline revealed his surprise at that condemnation. 'But you never once complained about Victorine—'

'And why would I have?' Emily got up in a sudden
movement, powered by angry defensiveness at that suggestion that she ought to have spoken up sooner. 'Why
would I have thought that complaining would have got me
anywhere with you? After all, you are not the world's most
sensitive person either, are you?'

A sardonic black brow quirked. 'Meaning?'

'Those portraits of Izabel in the salon, the dining room
and the main hall…' Emily illuminated tightly. 'I could've
understood that if you'd had children with her but you

didn't. How was I supposed to feel that the Quinta de Monteiro was *my* home?'

Duarte was studying her with frowning intensity but a faint perceptible pallor was spreading round his taut mouth. 'I never *thought*…I was so used to them being there—'

'Well, you know…your first wife may have been a great beauty and the paintings may be wonderful art, but you should've had them moved to less prominent places. I felt intimidated by them. And although I'm not terribly interested or indeed gifted in any way at fancy interior design and stuff like that,' Emily admitted flatly, 'I would've appreciated the freedom to redecorate just one room and feel that it, at least, was mine.'

Every bone in Duarte's lean dark devastating face was rigid by the time she had finished speaking. 'I cannot excuse myself for my lack of sensitivity.'

'No, you can't,' Emily agreed with very little in the way of satisfaction. Then nothing he said could touch or ease the hard knot of pain inside her. Even while she railed at him, she was thinking how pointless her reproaches were. Those oversights had merely spelt out his basic indifference to her feelings. He'd never been in love with her and only a man in love would have considered such things. But she'd said enough, knew that if she said anything more, he might realise just how jealous she'd been of his first wife. Not very nice, she reflected guiltily. Izabel had proved to be an impossible act to follow.

'It's all water under the bridge now.' Emily drew in a slow steadying breath, for she knew exactly what she needed to find peace of mind—her freedom. Freedom from such demeaning comparisons between herself and a dead woman. Freedom from wanting the love she could never have because that wanting was self-destructive. 'So, before you start telling me things you would much prefer not to tell me, *I* have something to say.'

'You have my full attention,' Duarte drawled in the most insidiously discouraging way.

'How do you do that?' Emily found herself asking. 'How do you manage always to make me feel that I shouldn't say what I'm about to say? I mean, you don't even *know* what I'm about to say!'

Duarte reached for her tense hands and unlaced them to hold her taut fingers in his. A bleak look had darkened his amazing eyes to a midnight glimmer of light as he gazed down at her. 'I'm not planning to smash any more doors down, *minha esposa*. Is that what is worrying you?'

The warmth of his hands on hers was a subtle entice-ment, as was the endearment. Pinned to the spot by those brilliant, dark, sexy eyes of his, she shivered, every tiny muscle she possessed tensing. That close, she could feel the heat of his lean powerful body, smell the evocative scent of him, composed of warm male laced with a faint hint of some exotic aftershave. All so familiar, all so devastatingly familiar that her senses reacted to him no matter what she did.

'I'm sorry if I frightened you. I lost control of my temper but it will not happen again,' Duarte intoned huskily, the very sound of his dark, deep voice setting up a quiver at the base of her spine.

'Stop it...' Emily urged shakily, desperately seeking to muster her defences against that wholly seductive onslaught of sensations.

'Stop...*what*?' Duarte probed with a sincere incompre-hension that infuriated her.

Her teeth gritted behind her compressed lips. She saw just how weak she was. It seemed she never learnt where he was concerned. He got close and her brain seemed to go into free fall—and yet he was still being cool and precise and he was not deliberately striving to set her wretched body alight. That knowledge just made her feel so horribly humiliated by her own lack of control that she dragged her hands free of his and stepped back.

'What's wrong?' Duarte murmured levelly. 'Are you still angry with me?'

Angry? Was she *still* angry? Mulling over that question, Emily conceded that she'd started being angry with Duarte within weeks of marrying him. Even while loving him to distraction, she'd been angry from the instant she laid her devastated eyes on Izabel's gorgeous photogenic face. Angry because she wasn't loved the same way, angry that her only value to him seemed to lie in supplying him with the child he wanted but angrier still that she was so hopelessly and helplessly obsessed with a man who neither needed nor loved her. In one way or another, she'd been made painfully conscious of that reality almost every day of their marriage.

'There's nothing wrong…' Emily said, not quite levelly. 'I just want a divorce.'

Duarte stilled the way people did when they got an entirely unexpected response. 'And you don't think that comes under the heading of there being something wrong?'

'Right now…' Emily breathed, colour highlighting her heart-shaped face, 'I do not want you getting clever with me.'

'Clever…' Duarte flung his proud, dark heard back.

Her fingers coiled into fists by her side as she forced herself on. 'I told you yesterday…I told you I didn't want to be your wife anymore—'

'Last night…' Duarte trailed out those two words until she felt like her face was burning, 'you gave me a rather different message.'

'I didn't know what was going on last night. I wasn't myself,' Emily stated between compressed lips of mortification. 'But that mistake is not going to make me change my mind about what's best for me—'

'Jamie?' Duarte slotted in, smooth as a stiletto.

Emily paled. 'I'm willing to live in Portugal so that you can see as much of Jamie as you like—'

'All right, you move out and I keep Jamie.'

Emily's lower lip parted company with her upper in sheer shock.

'Now I wonder why you aren't into that solution when it is only the reverse of what you are suggesting that *I* should accept,' Duarte pointed out without remorse. 'Only twenty-four hours after I get to meet my son, you want to deprive me of him again and you somehow expect me to be cool about it?'

'All right, you're making me feel horrible...' Emily muttered, unable to avoid seeing the unlovely comparison he'd put before her. 'But feeling as you do about me, you have no right to expect me to live with you just for Jamie's sake.'

'Haven't I? You were perfectly happy last night until I blew it,' Duarte reminded her without hesitation. 'Now, had you said then that you could not bear me to touch you, I would have agreed that at the very least we should separate.'

Emily caught on fast to that argument. Hugely aware that he could talk semantic circles round her and tie her into knots to the extent that she would soon not know where she was in the dialogue, she grasped hurriedly at the get-out clause he had put before her. 'Well, I'm saying it *now*. I can't bear for you to touch me!'

'Where do you get the nerve to say that to me?' Duarte derided, reacting to that statement with a level of incredulity that was seriously embarrassing.

Flushed to the roots of her red-gold hair, Emily backed off several steps. 'I'm not taking back a word of it...'

Like a leopard on the prowl, Duarte followed her retreat. 'I don't have to justify wanting a divorce—'

'Yes, you do,' Duarte overruled with infuriating logic.

'OK…' Trapped between the wall and Duarte's lean powerful physique, Emily came to a halt with her shoulderblades up hard against the plaster. 'When I married you, I was too young to know what I was doing. You took advantage of the fact that I was in love with you. I had a lousy hole-in-the-corner wedding and I didn't even get a honeymoon!'

Duarte elevated a winged black brow with pronounced disbelief. 'That's…*it*?'

'That's only to *begin* with!' Emily slung, her temper firing up fast at his refusal to take her seriously. 'Then you brought me home to a house ruled by your ex-mother-in-law, who hated me on sight. After that, you hardly bothered to notice that I was alive—'

A charismatic smile began to form on Duarte's wide, sensual mouth. 'I seem to recall noticing that you were alive so often and with such frequency that I once fell asleep in a board meeting!'

Chagrinned by that literal interpretation of her words, Emily changed tack to suit that line of argument as well. 'So you *admit* that all you ever shared with me was a bed—'

'If you wanted to share the board meetings too, you should have mentioned it.'

Pure rage filled Emily. 'When I phoned you during the day, you never once returned my calls!'

Duarte frowned. 'What calls?'

'I daresay there was a time or two when you were much too busy to speak to me but there is just no excuse for you never once phoning me back—'

'I never refused a call of yours in my life,' Duarte interrupted with a palpable edge of masculine annoyance. 'I have better manners. We Portuguese are not so taken up with business that we overlook either courtesy or family during working hours.'

'Well, I was overlooked time and time again until I got the message!' Emily raked back at him in a growing fury at her inability to make any charge stick and draw blood. 'And where were your precious manners when you failed to turn up for the dinner parties I arranged in my deadly boring, dutiful role of being your wife?'

'Again you are making false accusations, not one of which you have ever mentioned before,' Duarte condemned with chilling bite. 'Where is all this nonsense coming from and why have you wandered from the point?'

'*My* point is—' Emily stabbed the air between them with a raised hand and, even in the grip of her temper, was rather pleased with the effect.

Without warning, Duarte moved forward and brought his hands up to plant them on either side of her startled face, long fingers meshing into the strands of her fiery hair. Shimmering golden eyes that had the flashfire charge of lightning clashed with hers. '*Your* point is non-existent or else you might have said something worth listening to by now,' he grated rawly, half under his breath, as he gazed down at her. 'I asked you here so that we could talk in private and I could express my regrets for my behaviour last night. But you have refused to listen. Instead you have done nothing but sling lies at me!'

'Lies…?' Intimidated in a very physical way by the manner in which he had her cornered, Emily was nonetheless conscious of a sudden maddening and truly insane need for him to touch her in exactly the way she had told him minutes earlier that she could not *bear* to be touched.

'Desire is not a one-way street. I know when I am wanted by a woman,' Duarte spelt out in the same dark dangerous undertone that was playing merry hell with her awakened senses.

'Really? Absolutely always?' Emily framed doggedly but no longer quite sure of what she was saying and why.

Other reactions were taking over at mind-bending speed: the steady acceleration of her heartbeat, an alarming shortness of breath, a sensation of exhilaration and awareness so intense it was like standing on a razor edge.

Duarte laced his hand into a whole hank of fiery redgold strands to hold her fast and then he brought his hot hard mouth crashing down on hers. Fire in the hold, she thought crazily, every inch of her jolted by the surge of wild excitement charging her. He dropped his hands and inched up the skirt of her dress, long sure fingers gliding up over her slender thighs with a knowing eroticism that only added fuel to her response.

She was shaking, clinging to him. She did not know how or when her hands had crept up to grip his wide shoulders but only by holding on to him was she staying upright. With a sudden hungry groan, Duarte cupped his hands to her hips and lifted her against him, pushing her back against the wall, letting her feel the full force of his arousal. Any grip Emily had on reality vanished at that point.

She heard herself moan under his marauding mouth like an animal. With every invasive stab of his tongue he mimicked a infinitely more primal possession and stoked her desire to more electrifying heights.

'Duarte… Please,' she gasped.

'Please what?' Duarte probed huskily, pushing her thighs further apart, letting his expert fingers linger within inches of the throbbing core of her shivering body.

'You're torturing me!'

Duarte let her slide down the wall on to her own feet again and one of her shoes had fallen off, making her blink in confusion at the lopsided effect of her own stance.

'If I was a real bastard, I'd make you beg,' Duarte spelt out in a roughened undertone, spectacular golden eyes scorching over her as she struggled somewhat belatedly to haul her dress back down from her waist. 'But I'm far too excited to deny myself that long!'

'What are you *doing*?' Emily squeaked as he swept her up into his arms with more haste than ceremony.

'Emily…' Duarte groaned as he strode out of the drawing room and down the corridor towards the bedrooms. 'What do you *think* I'm doing?'

CHAPTER SEVEN

'BUT we were talking about getting a divorce!' Emily protested, sufficiently reanimated by the change of surroundings to say what she should have said five minutes sooner.

'Correction, *you* were talking on that subject. When you can put up some convincing resistance to my advances, I'll consider talking about it,' Duarte proffered with a wolfish and very male downward glance of challenge.

'I am not getting into bed with you again... It would be wrong!' Emily argued frantically as she shouldered open the door in a luxurious bedroom.

'Wrong at this juncture would be playing the tease and why should you want to?' Duarte enquired, lowering her to the carpet, bending down to pluck off the remaining shoe she wore so that she could stand normally and then spinning her round to unzip her dress.

As he spun her back like a doll and gave the sleeves of the garment a helpful tug to assist it on its downward journey, Emily stood as though transfixed. 'Duarte...I'm being serious—'

'So am I,' he swore, watching the dress slide down with satisfaction and shrugging out of his beautifully tailored jacket to let it fall on the carpet as well. 'I want you. Here. Now. Fast...'

'But you haven't even told me yet what you brought me to tell me...' her voice faltered and trailed away altogether as she thought of that 'here...now...fast' bit he had threatened and a truly unforgivable dart of liquid heat forced her to lock her knees together.

'I've done all the talking I want to do for one day. I've

apologised. I've owned up to gross insensitivity. You were as receptive as a rock-face but you didn't complain about anything I can't fix,' Duarte asserted on a very single-minded tack as he shed his tie and wrenched at his shirt with pronounced impatience.

'All right, I was lying when I said I didn't want you to touch me,' Emily owned up in desperation. 'But please keep your shirt on. If you take it off, I'm lost.'

Momentarily, Duarte paused and cast her a gleaming glance of vibrant amusement. He slid out of the shirt with the fluid grace of a matador in the bull ring. 'This is one battle you're destined to lose—'

'But I can't... We can't. This...*this* is not the answer!' Emily surveyed him with guilt-stricken intensity as he stood there poised, all hair-roughened bronzed skin and lean hard muscle. Him looking like a Greek god was not exactly the biggest help she'd ever received in her belief that she had to put a lid on what was happening between them.

'Isn't it?' Duarte reached out and hauled her into his arms, smouldering dark gaze roaming over the rise and fall of her breasts. He unclipped the bra, found a pouting swell of tormentingly sensitive flesh and rubbed his thumb over the throbbing tip. 'I want you so much I'm in agony...'

She leant into him even though she tried to stop herself. She could feel the same want mounting like a hungry, conscience-free flood inside her. Last night might never have happened. She was shocked at the strength of her own yearning, shocked by the overpowering surge of excitement awakened by the sight of his lean hand cupping her breast.

'This is what we need now, *minha esposa*,' Duarte asserted, pulling into him and lifting her to bring her down on the side of the elegant sleigh bed. 'Talking is too dangerous. Talking when there is no solution is just stupid.'

Hearing those sentiments pronounced with such unquenchable masculine conviction should have sent her leaping from his arms in angry frustration. But he was arranging her on the bed with the care of a male about to extract the utmost from the experience and she could not take her eyes from his. Dear heaven, those wonderful eyes. He just had to look at her and her own thoughts just dwindled and yet somehow she felt secure about that, safe. That was all wrong and she knew it was but when Duarte loomed over her like every fantasy she'd ever had, self-control was not an option her overheated body wanted to consider.

'Talking is supposed to *be* the solution,' she murmured in a last attempt to place head over heart.

'It put us in separate beds last night. It made me kick in a door. You think that's healthy?' Duarte challenged as he stripped down to a pair of black silk boxer shorts that were the very last word in sexy apparel. 'No, my way is better.'

My way is better. Not exactly the last word in compromise, was he? But she gazed up at him and the most enormous swell of love surged through her and, all of a sudden, nothing else mattered.

'Once, you used to look at me like that all the time.' Duarte came down on the bed like a predator, taking his time, and a helpless little shiver of anticipation rippled through her taut and restive limbs. 'I became accustomed to it…'

Most men would be pretty content to be uncritically adored by their wives, Emily reflected. And the ironic truth was, while she'd remained content to settle for less on her own behalf, she had been happier. Whether he knew it or not, the wild card that had upset the balance had been the very unsettling discovery that he had loved Izabel. No, nobody had told her that; even at her worst, Victorine hadn't been that cruel. She had seen it in that wedding photograph of Izabel and Duarte together, the love, pride and satisfaction he had had in his acquisition of his beautiful bride.

'I want it back,' Duarte said lazily and he pressed his wide, sensual mouth to the tiny pulse below her ear, a sensitive spot that seemed to overreact with blinding enthusiasm and sent her momentarily haywire with hunger.

Gasping for breath and trying to sound cool, Emily looked up at him and trying to sound dry but actually sounding very stressed, she said, 'I don't do adoration any more. I grew up.'

Duarte let a provocative hand roam over her distended nipples and her back arched as if he had burned her. 'But you can regress,' he murmured smooth as silk.

Regressing felt so darned good, she thought helplessly. He pushed her flat again with a husky laugh of amusement and lowered his carnal mouth to her tingling breasts where he turned torment into a new art form. Control evaporated about there for Emily. Her body was all liquid burning heat powered by a hunger that was steadily overwhelming her.

'You want me?' Duarte demanded, fierce control etched in his dark features.

'Now...' she begged.

He spread her thighs like a Viking invader set on sexual plunder and it still wasn't fast enough for her. He came over her, into her, in a shocking surge of primal male power and she almost passed out at the wave of intense pleasure.

'You feel like hot silk,' he groaned with raw sensual appreciation, plunging deeper still.

And from then on in, she gave herself up to voluptuous abandonment. The hot sweet pleasure just took over and she could only breathe in short agonised gasps. In the steely grip of that mounting excitement, her heart thundering, her blood racing like wildfire through her veins, she whimpered and arched her hips to invite his urgent thrusts. She cried out at the peak of a climax of breathtaking power, her entire body wrenched into the explosive hold of that erotic release.

Afterwards, it was like coming back to life after a long time somewhere else. Where else, Emily could not have specified at that precise moment, but it didn't seem to matter for she felt this glorious sense of unquestioning contentment and delight. Her needs felt few; she was with Duarte and Duarte was with her. Life felt wonderful.

Duarte rolled over, carrying her with him, and gazed down at her passion-stunned face with brilliant golden eyes of satisfaction. 'I think that settles the divorce question for the foreseeable future.'

Disorientated by that sudden descent to the prosaic and the provocative when her own brain was still floating in euphoric clouds, she blinked and stared up at him. Duarte pushed her head down into his shoulder, dropped what felt like a kiss on the crown of her head and held her close in silence.

'Duarte?' she mumbled, trying to ground her brain and focus.

'I'm going over to London on business next week. You and Jamie can come and we'll visit your family...OK?'

Thrown by that suggestion, Emily began to lift her head.

'I was bloody furious when I discovered you'd gone there and they'd thrown you out again,' Duarte stated, startling her even more, his strong jawline clenching. 'Not very sympathetic, were they?'

Emily had paled. 'I hadn't got around to telling them about us being separated...or anything else,' she mumbled, shrinking from any mention of that episode with Toby. 'Mum and Dad just didn't think it was right that I had left you and they probably thought that showing me the door again would send me back to Portugal more quickly.'

'Or maybe they thought that helping you might offend *me*,' Duarte drawled very quietly. 'And that if they offended me, I might not be just so generous in putting new business in the way of the family firm. Have you even considered that angle?'

Emily regarded him with shaken reproach. 'Is that how you think of my family? That's an *awful* thing to suggest!'

'I'm an appalling cynic but, obviously, you would know your own flesh and blood best...' Duarte murmured, relieving her with the ease with which he made that concession.

Emily relaxed again.

'It's just that most parents would think twice before they threw a married, very pregnant and distressed daughter back out into the snow,' Duarte continued, dismaying her with his persistence. 'They also took my side. They didn't even *know* what my side was but they took it all the same—'

'People don't always react the way you expect them to...especially when you take them by surprise, as I did,' Emily pointed out defensively.

'I can certainly second that.'

He didn't like her parents. Why had she never realised that before? Emily lay there in his arms, forced to reluctantly concede that, if anything, the emotional distance between her and her parents had only grown since her marriage and had been almost severed altogether when she turned up on the doorstep without her husband in tow eight months earlier. Her family had visited her only once in Portugal. Although Emily had bent over backwards to ensure their every comfort and provide every possible entertainment, true enjoyment had seemed to elude her relatives. Her mother and her sisters had seemed to band together in a trio of constant criticism which had made Emily feel about an inch high. The couple of invitations she had made after that had been turned down with no great effort devoted to polite excuses.

'Let's have lunch and then go home and spend the rest

of the day with Jamie,' Duarte suggested, taking her mind off her regret over her uneasy relationship with the family she loved.

'That's a lovely idea,' she said warmly.

Only then did it cross her mind that she'd come to the city apartment expecting to hear some ghastly revelation that had never transpired. Desperate to conserve her own pride, she'd started rambling on about getting a divorce when a divorce was probably the very last thing in the world that she wanted. Sometimes, she worked herself up into such a state, she acknowledged shame-facedly. Duarte had made passionate love to her twice in twenty-four hours. Was that the behaviour of a man interested in another woman? And wouldn't she have made the biggest mistake of her life in saying no? They had achieved a closeness that had entirely eluded them the night before.

They lunched in the elegant dining room and were just finishing their coffee prior to departing when the door opened without any warning and Bliss strolled in carrying a document case.

'I'm sorry, Duarte. I didn't realise that your wife was here. Mrs Monteiro...'

'Miss Jarrett,' Emily muttered, barely able to look at the blonde after the unpleasantness of their meeting earlier in the day.

But Duarte was already rising from his chair, his charismatic smile lighting up his darkly handsome features. 'My apologies, Bliss. I changed my plans and neglected to inform you.'

A dewy smile free of her usual mockery fixed to her exquisite face, Bliss sighed softly, 'I really ought to be used to that by now.'

'I'm going home for the rest of the day.'

Emily watched the little tableau playing out in front of her with wide eyes of disconcertion. She saw Duarte stride to greet Bliss and receive the document case rather than wait for her to come to him as he once would have done. Duarte was, as a rule, formal with his employees and un- given to addressing them by their first names. When had he decided to relax his formidable reserve with Bliss?

'I'll see you out,' Duarte assured Bliss.

As they left the room together, Emily sat like a stone in her chair for several seconds. Just when had such a stag- gering change taken place in Duarte's relationship with his executive assistant? Unable to sit still, she found herself getting up and walking restively over to the window. She recalled Bliss's low soft voice, a tone she'd never heard the blonde employ before and she'd never seen her smile like that either, like an infinitely more feminine version of the harder-edged Bliss she herself had got to know. Out of nowhere, a tension headache settled round Emily's temples like a tightening circle of steel. Thump, thump, thump was her body's enervated response to the mental alarm bell go- ing off at shrieking decibels inside her head.

Duarte and Bliss? Were her suspicions insane? Was she even thinking straight? But hadn't Bliss carefully ended their friendship only a few hours earlier? Hadn't Bliss made it clear that her sympathies now lay squarely with Duarte? And, finally, hadn't Bliss venomously pointed out that Duarte might already have another woman in his life?

Was Bliss that other woman? Her tummy churning at the very thought of such a development, Emily struggled to get a grip on her flailing emotions. She felt like a truck had run over her. She felt cold inside and out. Why shouldn't Duarte be attracted to Bliss? Bliss was beautiful and witty and clever. Bliss was exactly the kind of wife Duarte should have picked to replace Izabel. Was he sleeping with her? *Had* he slept with her? Exactly when had his relationship with his executive assistant become so familiar that he smiled at her like that? Smiled with warmth and approval and intimacy?

Was she crazy to be thinking these kind of thoughts? There they were, calling each other by their first names and exchanging smiles, and suddenly she had them tucked up in bed together? She was not going to leap in and say anything to Duarte. She was *not*. Any such questions would be very much resented.

And while she stood there, fighting to put a lid on her emotional turmoil, she found herself thinking back to her friendship with Bliss Jarrett. Within months of her marriage to a male who worked very long hours, Emily had become very lonely. Although she'd been dragged out everywhere by Victorine on social visits and had met several women whom she might have become friendly with, the language barrier had reigned supreme. She'd met very few people who spoke fluent English and it had taken her a long time to master even the basics of Portuguese.

When she had phoned Duarte's office, she had always been put through to Bliss. She would leave a message with Bliss but Duarte would never call back. Once or twice in those early days, she had phoned just to check that her message had been passed on to him. With an audible suggestion of embarrassed sympathy on Emily's behalf, Bliss would gently assure her that her husband had received the message.

Eventually they had begun chatting and Emily had confided that she hated shopping alone. Bliss had offered to accompany her and then hastily retracted the suggestion with the apologetic explanation that Duarte would not approve of his wife socialising with a mere employee. Desperate for company, Emily had pointed out that what Duarte didn't know wouldn't hurt him.

And so the friendship that she had valued had begun, a friendship that was a breath of fresh air to someone as lonely and insecure as she had been then. Shopping trips, lunches and, on several occasions when Duarte was abroad on business, Bliss had invited her to her apartment for a meal. There she had met Toby and there she had come up with the stupid childish plan to have her portrait painted in the forlorn hope of displacing an image of Izabel from even one wall of the *quinta*.

'Are you ready?' Duarte asked from the dining room doorway, making her jerk and return to the present.

Emily breathed in deep, steadying herself. She would make no comment; she would say nothing. There was probably nothing whatsoever in what she had seen. It was only her own insecurity playing tricks on her imagination. Crazily she pictured herself standing up at a divorce hearing and saying 'Duarte *smiled* at her…that's my evidence.'

In the lift that took them down to the ground floor, Emily stole a glance that spread and lingered to encompass every visible inch of her tall, dark and absolutely gorgeous husband. She loved him. They were back together…weren't they? He was making an effort to repair the great yawning cracks in their marriage, wasn't he? So what if most of the effort he was putting in was bedroom-orientated? Did that matter? Did that make him less committed? Had he *ever* been committed to her?

Engaged in such frantic and feverish thoughts, Emily tripped over a metal bin to the side of the exit, skidded across the floor and came down on her bottom.

'*Meu Deus!*' Duarte exclaimed and immediately reached for her to help her to her feet again. 'Are you all right?'

'So…s-so,' she stammered, refusing to massage the throbbing ache assailing her bruised hip.

'Didn't you see it?' Smoothing her down, Duarte focused on the bin which was about four feet tall and hard to miss.

Emily clambered into the limousine on wobbly legs. She would keep her tongue between her teeth for the whole drive home. Just then, she recalled that odd little scene she had witnessed at the airport between Duarte and Bliss. The way he had taken a few extra minutes to speak to Bliss in private before joining Emily in the car, the tension she'd witnessed between them. What had he been saying to Bliss to make her freeze and turn red? Exactly how intimate were they?

'When did you get so friendly with Bliss Jarrett?' That demand just erupted out of Emily's mouth and she was horrified at herself, at the clumsiness of that leading question, not to mention its undeniably accusing tone.

There was one of those truly awful laden silences.

Duarte elevated a sardonic brow and his spiky black lashes partially screened his dark deepset gaze. 'I don't think that's a subject we should open.'

What the heck was that supposed to mean? An evasive response was the very last thing she needed, in the mood she was in, but she really did try very hard to let the subject stay closed. She bit down on her tongue so hard, she tasted her own blood. She told herself that she ought to trust him but, the trouble was, she knew she no longer trusted Bliss. And even though Duarte was emanating sufficient vibes to warn her off, she ignored them.

'It's natural for me to be curious.'

'I'm not sure that you'll be grateful for my explanation. Bliss was very embarrassed when she realised that you had had an affair with her cousin and she offered to resign,' Duarte advanced in a glacial tone.

'Did she really?' Emily whispered shakily, feeling like he had just dropped a giant suffocating rock on top of her.

'After those developments, it would have been a little difficult for us to return to our former working relationship as though nothing had happened. I have great respect for Bliss both as an employee and a personal friend. I would appreciate it if you would keep that fact in mind.'

'I'm not really sure what you're saying,' Emily mumbled although she was dreadfully afraid that she did. She was also horribly tempted to say that, in terms of personal friendship, Bliss spread herself around behind other people's backs, but it sounded mean and petty and she stopped herself just in time.

Duarte angled his proud dark head back and viewed her with chilling dark eyes without the smallest shade of warmer gold. 'You have no right to question me. You had an affair. You broke up our marriage. You then vanished and it was seven months before an investigator even picked up on your trail—'

'Duarte…' she broke in jaggedly, her voice breaking under that onslaught.

'Throughout those months I didn't know whether you were dead or alive or even whether or not I *was* actually a father. It was a very difficult time for me. During that period, Bliss became something more than just an employee—she became a supportive friend.' His beautiful dark eyes were like a card-player's eyes, remote, cool, but disturbingly challenging.

She wanted to kill him. Then she wanted to strangle herself. He was telling her the cruellest thing. He was telling her that her own behaviour, her stupid immature vanishing act and all those months of silence had laid the foundations of what he termed a 'friendship'. Was he telling her that Bliss was his mistress and that he wasn't giving her up? And was it unjust and melodramatic of her to suspect that Bliss might have a far more ambitious agenda than mere friendship in mind? Hadn't Bliss frightened Emily into leaving Portugal and then made use of that opportunity to increase her own standing with Duarte? Or was, Emily asked herself, she trying to justify her *own* mistakes and blame Bliss for the fall-out?

At that point what felt like the last piece of a bewildering puzzle seemed to fall into dismaying place and Emily stared at Duarte in sudden horror. 'Bliss is that third party you mentioned, *isn't* she? That discreet person who confirmed that I was carrying on with Toby when I *wasn't*—'

'I won't dignify that accusation with an answer,' Duarte countered drily.

It was as if he was slamming a door in her face without conscience. She wanted to ask him how intimate his relationship with Bliss had become but was not entirely sure she could stand to hear an honest answer at that moment. He would not feel that he had to defend himself. After all, didn't he believe that she had betrayed him with Toby first? She could feel his anger, contained but always there between them, awakened by the reminder of her supposed affair, his attitude hardened by the manner in which she had questioned him about Bliss.

'Tell me,' she muttered dry-mouthed, feeling that no matter where she turned she was in a no-win situation and always in the wrong, 'would you even have considered bringing me back to Portugal had I not had Jamie?'

'The jury's still very much out on that one,' Duarte drawled with freezing cool. 'Right now, I'm changing direction like a metronome.'

Neither of them said another word for the remainder of the drive back to the *quinta*.

After they arrived Duarte strode off with the terse explanation that he had an important call to make, Emily went upstairs to fetch Jamie and scooped him out of his cot with eager hands. After stopping for a chat with the nanny and discussing at some length the reality that her son needed more clothes, she cuddled Jamie all the way down to the ground floor again. There she set him on a rug in the salon to talk to him.

'Your father doesn't like me very much right now but that's OK,' Emily informed her six-month-old son with a rather wooden bright smile, destined to reassure him that she really wasn't sad. 'I'm just warning you that whenever you do anything stupid, it will come back and haunt you for a good hundred years. It will smack you in the face at every turn and leave you feeling awful—'

'I think you're taxing his concentration span...' Duarte murmured from somewhere behind her at the same time as she noticed that Jamie was kicking his feet and demonstrating definite signs of excited welcome at the approach of someone he liked.

'I didn't know you were there!' Emily was seriously rattled by his appearance.

'Put on the fake smile again. Jamie's not very discerning.' Duarte hunkered down by her side to grasp their son's extended chubby fingers. 'He wouldn't know a pity-fest from a celebration.'

'If that's supposed to make me feel better—'

'No...but *this* is...' Anchoring one powerful hand into her tumbling hair, Duarte tugged her head around and captured her startled lips under his. Instinctively, she began to tip towards him. That slow-burning kiss awakened a bone-deep yearning inside her for the pure reassurance of physical contact and acceptance.

And then something funny happened. Her memory threw up a perfect recollection of his last words before they vacated the car. Just as quickly, she found herself pulling back from him for the first time in her life and she caught the flash of surprise in his stunning gaze before he veiled it.

'If I'm only here for Jamie's benefit, we'd better not stretch me too thin,' she said tightly.

Duarte reached forward and lifted their son with the same carefulness he might have utilised in handling a bomb. And her heart twisted because she knew it was her fault that he was still afraid of being rejected by Jamie. Emily being

Emily, she then felt immediately horrible for not allowing Duarte to kiss her as much as he wanted to.

'Victorine tells me that you invited her to stay on,' Duarte murmured while he struggled to get Jamie into a comfortable position on one raised, lean, powerful thigh. 'In the circumstances that was extremely generous of you. However, she's asked me if she can move into a house on the outskirts of the estate which is currently unoccupied. I've agreed.'

'With me in charge, prepare yourself for a sudden slump in staff efficiency,' Emily told him apprehensively.

'If there's a problem, you come to me and I will deal with it.'

Meanwhile Jamie chortled and dug delighted hands into Duarte's luxuriant black hair and pulled hard.

'He's not scared of me any more,' Duarte breathed with a sudden grin.

Duarte took Jamie upstairs to the picture gallery which was lined with distinctly gloomy canvases of Monteiro ancestors and gave their infant son a potted history of the family with a perfectly straight face.

'Don't you think he's just a little young for this?' Emily remarked.

'This is our family. Nothing comes before family. Not business, not anything,' Duarte imparted with considerable gravity. 'My earliest memory is of my father bringing me here and telling me what it means to be a Monteiro.'

Not noticeably impressed, Jamie went to sleep draped over Duarte's shoulder. When Emily came back downstairs from settling their son for a nap, three estate workers were engaged in removing Izabel's giant portrait from the wall in the salon. The whole room would have to be redecorated. She wondered where the painting was going, looked at that gorgeous sultry face and sighed to herself. For so long, she had tormented herself with pointless comparisons between herself and Duarte's first wife. Now she was receiving what would seem to be her just reward. She now had live competition that struck her as much more threatening.

Nothing comes before family, Duarte had stated with unequivocable conviction. Finally he had answered that loaded question she had shot at him in the car. Jamie came first, so therefore Jamie's needs would take priority over more personal inclinations and mothers were not interchangeable. But where did Bliss fit into that picture?

That night she lay in her bed watching the door which had been expertly repaired stay resolutely closed. She was not one whit surprised. Duarte had been angry when she turned away from him during that kiss. Duarte would sooner burn alive than give her a second such opportunity. He was so damnably proud and stubborn.

So there you are, once again you did the wrong thing, Emily told herself wretchedly. Here she was worrying that the man she loved might be, at the very least, seriously attracted to a woman who was on convenient call for him throughout his working day. And what had Emily done? Angry with him, striving to protect her own pride, she had rejected him and she could not have picked a worse time to do it…

CHAPTER EIGHT

FIVE days later, on the afternoon of the party which Bliss had organised, Emily was fiddling in desperation with a vast floral arrangement in the main hall.

Victorine had been creative with flowers. Emily was not. In spite of all her efforts, the blooms looked like they'd been dropped from a height into the huge glass vase and persisted in standing like soldiers on parade when what she really wanted them to do was *bend*.

The past five days had been an ongoing punishment. The long-awaited removal of Izabel's portraits had left ghastly marks on the panelling in the main hall and on the wall-paper in the dining room and the salon. As there wasn't time for redecoration, she'd attempted to move the furniture around, which hadn't worked very well. In the end she'd taken paintings from other places to try and cover up the damage. At one stage she had been tearing her hair out to such an extent she had even seriously contemplated approaching Duarte and begging for Izabel's wretched portraits to be brought back from wherever they had gone...on a temporary basis. Only the prospect of his incredulity at such an astonishing request had prevented her.

Her mood was not improved by the reality that she and Duarte were existing in a state of armed neutrality in which her bedroom door stayed closed and might even be left to gather cobwebs. That was not good for her nerves. Last night she'd decided that even having it smashed down in what now seemed like true *heroic* style wouldn't make her bat an eyelash and would indeed be welcomed.

Meanwhile, Duarte was being teeth-clenchingly courteous and charming, his entire demeanour that of a male wholly untouched by anything so uncool as a desire for the smallest physical contact with his wife. She knew he would not break...at least, not in her direction. At the same time she had the dubious comfort of knowing that Bliss was rarely out of his reach. At her lowest moments, Emily wondered if he was already slaking his high sex-drive with the glamorous blonde and even if Duarte and Bliss could have been secret lovers long before Toby came into Emily's life...

Indeed, her imagination had taken her to the outer reaches of her worst nightmares. In those worst-case scenarios, Duarte figured as the biggest four-letter word on planet Earth and behaved with Machiavellian cunning and cruelty to deceive his dumb, stupid wife. Now she was finding herself recalling her own trusting friendship with Bliss's cousin, Toby Jarrett.

'It's so simple,' Bliss had laughed. 'You want Izabel's portraits out of the way, you have yourself painted and present your husband with the canvas as a gift. He is certain to take the hint.'

But Bliss had had an uphill battle persuading Emily that she was worthy of being painted. To sit for her own portrait had required a level of self-esteem that Emily did not possess. However, in the end Emily had allowed herself to be convinced and, by then, Toby had already been renting a tiny house and studio in the village below the *quinta*.

They had first met at Bliss's apartment. He'd had his girlfriend with him, a wealthy and possessive divorcée who did not trust other women within an inch of Toby's blond good looks and easy boyish charm. But Toby had never flirted with Emily when she went down to his studio for sittings. His lady friend had soon tired of superintending Emily's visits like a suspicious chaperone.

With Toby living so close to the Quinta de Monteiro,

Emily had felt it was only polite to invite him to dine with her and Duarte one evening. So she had told her first lie to Duarte and had pretended that she had just got talking to the young Englishman in the village. Prevented from revealing her friendship with Bliss, how could she possibly have told the truth? And, since she'd wanted the portrait to be a big surprise, she had had to keep her visits to Toby's studio a secret.

After a meal during which her husband and Toby seemed to radically disagree on virtually every subject under the sun, Duarte had drawled, 'Try to bury him in a larger gathering of guests if you invite him again. He's as argumentative as a rebellious teenager and, if he's such a wonderful artist, why did he drop out of his art college in England?'

Duarte had been extremely unimpressed by Toby. Emily, by then in the early stages of pregnancy and suffering from horrible morning sickness and a distinct feeling of abandonment because Duarte had not made love to her in weeks, had felt defiant. Whatever else, Toby might be, he was, in Emily's humble opinion, an incredibly talented painter. As far as she was concerned, any artist who could make her look almost beautiful was gifted beyond belief. She'd looked forward to the prospect of Duarte being forced to eat his own words.

Nobody had been more astonished than Emily that fatal night when Toby suddenly broke into an impassioned speech on the terrace beyond the salon. Telling her that he loved her, that Duarte did not deserve her, that if she ran away with him, he would cherish her forever and never neglect her as Duarte did. Since Emily had seen no warning signs of Toby falling in love with her, she'd been transfixed by shock. The most enormous self-pity had engulfed her when she appreciated that, for the very first time ever, someone was telling her that they *loved* her. Duarte, she'd thought in an agony of regret that evening, would never

ever look at her that way or speak to her as though she was some unutterably precious being whom he could not live without.

'*Meu Deus...*' Duarte breathed without the smallest warning from behind Emily.

Dredged at dismaying speed from her miserable recollections of the past, Emily turned scarlet because even *thinking* about Toby made Emily feel ultra-guilty. She spun round to find Duarte, sleek and sophisticated in a superb dark business suit, engaged in studying her floral arrangement with raised dark brows.

'Was the vase knocked over?' Duarte enquired.

Emily paled and surveyed the results of her creative efforts with tragic eyes and a sense of injustice. Bad had gone to worse. Several stems had broken beneath her too-rough handling and the blooms now hung forlorn.

'No, the vase didn't fall,' Emily admitted in a small, wooden voice devoid of any human emotion. 'I was trying to arrange the flowers.'

Beside her, she heard Duarte draw in an audible breath. 'I was looking at it from the wrong angle. It's one of those trendy displays...right?'

'Oh, shut up!' Emily launched at him, shocking him as much as she shocked herself with that outburst that rejected his face-saving excuse. She dashed a defensive hand across eyes that were now filled with stinging tears. 'It looks blasted awful and you *know* it does! I'm no good with flowers—'

'Why should you be?'

'Because other women are and I'm no good at *anything*!' Emily lamented bitterly and went racing for the stairs before she broke down altogether. On the first wide landing, she glanced back over her shoulder. Towards the back of the hall, Duarte's uniformed chauffeur, who was holding a pile of fancy-looking gift boxes, stood like a graven image.

Duarte was just staring up at her with stunned dark eyes that seemed to suggest that not only was she lousy in the feminine creativity stakes but also decidedly unhinged.

Emily fled on up the stairs like a lemming gathering speed to jump off a cliff. Why not? A night of horrible humiliation stretched before her. Playing hostess with Bliss smirking on the sidelines at her awkwardness. The even more horrendous challenge of choosing what to wear. The crazy but superstitious conviction that having her predecessor's portraits banished had been the kind of move calculated to bring serious bad luck.

Therefore, it was decidedly disorientating for Emily to race for the sanctuary of her bedroom and find the bed stripped, the wardrobe doors hanging open on empty spaces and two maids engaged on a thorough clean-up. Slowly she backed away again, only to find something or someone very solid blocking her retreat. She whirled round, trembling, shaken, bewildered by what she had just seen.

'Calm down,' Duarte spread eloquent hands in a soothing motion.

'Calm down? Where am I being moved to now? Out the front door? Or down to the cellars with the rats?'

'Let's not get totally carried away, Emily. There are no rats in the Monteiro wine cellars.' Duarte made what she considered to be a totally unnecessary contradiction.

'But there *is* one upstairs!'

Duarte frowned. 'You are joking, I hope—'

'Why are you always so literal? I'm referring to you!' she hissed in frustration.

Duarte tried to reach for her hand. She folded her arms but he was persistent. Unfolding them by the means of gentle pressure, he imprisoned one of her hands in his. Then he dragged her down the corridor, across two landings and all the way over to the other side of the house. Nothing short of thumbscrews would have squeezed a demand to know where he was taking her from Emily's mutinously compressed lips.

Duarte cast open the door of his own bedroom, indeed threw it dramatically wide. Emily stalked in, seething with so many uncontrolled emotions she was afraid she might explode.

'Now look around you,' Duarte suggested, sounding just a little taut.

Her teddy nightshirt was spread across one corner of his bed like a major statement. 'But...b-but, we've *never* shared a room—'

'Any reason why we shouldn't?'

Straying away from him, thrown into a loop by this unexpected development, Emily plucked her nightshirt off the bed, embarrassed that it had been put on show when it was so very unworthy of public display.

'Is that a...no?'

Emily shrugged and rubbed the fringe on the rug with the toe of her canvas-shod foot. But in the depths of the eyes she kept tactfully lowered lurked surprised satisfaction. Indeed, it was amazing how powerful she felt at that moment. He would have done *anything* sooner than ask up front. She could feel his tension. A non-verbal invitation to share a marital bed was quite a proclamation of intent on his part and a none-too-subtle step in the right direction. Suddenly the past five days of dreadful stress she had suffered while attempting to seem unconcerned by the divisions between them seemed very worthwhile—ultimately, *he* had come to *her*.

'It's a big bed,' Emily acknowledged softly. 'I suppose we can be as frigidly polite in that bed as we are at the dinner table.'

'OK,' he murmured with a level of cool that almost made her smile. 'By the way, I've bought you a present.'

Emily was stuffing the nightshirt into as small a ball as

possible and endeavouring to lose it discreetly by pushing it with a prodding toe below the bed. 'A...*present*?'

Duarte indicated the gilded boxes now stacked two feet high on the dressing table.

'For...*me*?' Emily hurried over to the stack to investigate with great curiosity. Never before had Duarte given her a surprise gift.

She hauled all the boxes over to the bed. The lid of the biggest one went flying and she ripped into the tissue paper and was astonished to emerge with some sort of garment. 'You bought me...something to wear?'

'For the party tonight.'

'Why would you buy me something to wear?' Emily asked in sincere bewilderment.

Duarte elbowed back his well-cut jacket and dug two lean hands into his trouser pockets and shifted a wide shoulder in an understated shrug. 'A whim...'

She shook out the incredibly tiny garment. 'But it looks like...' She bit back the tactless word, 'underwear', and studied the fine glistening fabric with wide questioning eyes.

'A dress?' he suggested.

'A...d-dress?' she stammered, striving valiantly to conceal her horror at the prospect of appearing in public with bare arms, legs on display and nothing whatsoever to draw attention away from her non-existent bosom. 'But it's too small to be a dress...'

Duarte breathed in deep.

'And it's so *pale* in colour.' A sort of delicate palest blue that was certain to make her naturally fair skin look washed-out and ghostly.

'Maybe this wasn't one of my better ideas,' Duarte remarked in a rather strained undertone.

Dear heaven, she was being so cruelly tactless! He finally made the effort to go and buy her an unexpected and per-

sonal gift and she stood around moaning about it like an
ungrateful brat. If he wanted her to appear with every
skinny bone accentuated, she would do so. If he wanted
her to wear a dustbin bag, she would try to wear it with a
smile. It was the thought which counted, not the actual gift.

With forced enthusiasm she dug into the remainder of
the boxes, terrified of what other horrors awaited her. Shoes
to match but so flat, she would disappear; only two-inch
high heels, she noted in dismay. Lingerie fine enough to
flow through the proverbial wedding ring alongside the
dress but at least while she was shivering, she would be
benefiting from an extra layer. An unpadded bra…how
could he? Was nothing sacrosanct?

Strolling over, Duarte extended a large jewel case. 'Sapphires to go with the dress.'

She froze as if a spectral hand had danced down her
spine. As he flipped open the case to display a gorgeous
necklace and drop earrings, Emily exuded discomfiture
rather than pleasure. 'Did Izabel…ever wear them?' she
whispered haltingly.

'No…I have *never* asked you to wear anything worn by
Izabel!' Duarte grated in a seriously rattled response.

'But I thought…you know? All that jewellery you
shoved at me just after we got married…I thought it had
belonged to her.'

Duarte looked heavenward as if praying for self-control.
'Izabel only ever wore diamonds and Victorine has them
now. I gave you the family jewellery, not one piece of
which Izabel liked.'

'Well, I wish you'd told me that a long time ago…'
Emily admitted tremulously, now willing to stretch out a
shy fingertip to touch the gleaming beauty of a single sap-
phire. For her, just for *her*. She could hardly believe it. She
swallowed the great fat lump forming in her throat and
blinked back tears

'I may have my flaws but I am not *that* insensitive.'

They were talking about Izabel quite naturally, Emily registered in surprise. He was finally talking about Izabel instead of going horribly silent and bleak and avoiding the subject.

'I'm really touched that you should go to all this effort just for me,' Emily said chokily but she hoped, where the dress and the bra were concerned, he wasn't planning to make a habit of spontaneous shopping trips on her behalf.

'It's an effort that I should have made a lot sooner than this,' Duarte breathed almost harshly.

'Better late than never...' Emily mumbled, pretty much stunned by that admission of fault. She felt even guiltier that she had never worn any of the jewellery he had given her after their marriage because she'd honestly believed it had all been Izabel's. She must have seemed so ungrateful, she thought now.

She took a deep breath. 'I think I ought to admit that I've always been terribly jealous of Izabel.'

'Jealous?' Duarte awarded her a startled look.

Emily winced. 'She got the wedding dress and the honeymoon. She was so beautiful and really gifted at decorating—'

'She hired top designers—'

'And being a hostess—'

'She hired the best caterers—'

Emily frowned, for he was denting the mystic myth of Izabel and she could not understand why he should be so disloyal to her predecessor's memory. 'Obviously, she was special. You fell in love with her when you were only a teenager—'

Duarte vented a grim laugh that silenced her. 'Please don't tell me that you listened to Victorine's story about Izabel and I having been childhood sweethearts!'

'Well, yes...but—'

Seeing her confusion, Duarte groaned out loud, his lean strong face bleak. 'You really don't know the truth even now, do you? But then, who would go out of their way to tell you the sordid details? I didn't want to relive them and Victorine always preferred to inhabit a dream world where her daughter was concerned.'

'Sordid details?' Emily queried in bewilderment. 'What are you talking about?'

'Izabel was a drug addict and not one who had any desire to be cured.'

Feeling the bed hit the back of her knees, Emily dropped down on it in a state of shock. 'You're not serious...'

Recognising her disbelief, Duarte expelled his breath on a hiss. And then he told her about Izabel. Yes, he had first met her when he was sixteen but Izabel had been five years older and quite out of his reach. Indeed he had not met her again until he was in his twenties. An heiress in her own right, Izabel's father had died when she was a child and she'd been raised by her adoring mother and allowed unlimited freedom from an early age.

'Unfortunately, I didn't move in Izabel's world, nor did I know her circle of friends. While they were partying, I was studying and then working eighteen-hour days in the bank. When I met her again six years later, I was mad for her,' Duarte admitted bluntly. 'I couldn't believe that she was still single. I couldn't wait to marry her; I just couldn't believe how *lucky* I was...'

Emily studied the rug at her feet. She really didn't want the intimate details, but they washed off her again because her mind was still fighting to handle the concept of the glamorous Izabel as an addict.

'I caught her with cocaine on the second day of our honeymoon. She just laughed, called me a killjoy and said I had better get used to it because that was how she lived. I was shattered,' Duarte confessed with grim exactitude. 'Before the wedding, I *had* seen her in a very excitable state but I didn't recognise her behaviour as abnormal or suspect the truth. She did have a very lively personality…and she was a tremendous show-off.'

'A…show-off?' Emily's own misconceptions about Izabel were sunk into final obscurity by that almost wry label.

'Izabel craved attention and publicity. No matter what it took, she had to be noticed and admired. She was the ultimate party girl.'

'Couldn't you persuade her to accept professional help?'

'Four times in three years she was rushed into hospital with overdoses. Neither the doctors, nor I, nor even her mother could talk her into entering a rehabilitation clinic or even considering a treatment plan. Mentally, she went downhill fast—but addicts have a distorted grip on reality—'

'Surely other people must've realised she was taking drugs?'

'When she did anything crazy, her friends would cover up for her because they had the same habits to protect and conceal. She had her own money, dealers in every port of call and any relationship we had fell apart within months. My sister Elena died because I was unable to control Izabel.'

Duarte's restive hands moved in a small silent motion that just screamed guilt and more pain than Emily had ever witnessed in another human being.

'I don't believe that. I *don't* believe it was your fault!' Emily protested fiercely.

'When I was abroad, Elena would try to watch over Izabel, for Victorine was quite unequal to the task. My twin made the fatal mistake of getting into Izabel's car and letting her drive. The car went off the road at the most phenomenal speed…' he completed thickly.

'Please don't think of this or talk about it any more,'

Emily begged, humbled by the agony he could not hide and appalled by what she had learnt. She was devastated that he had contrived to bury what could only have been a three-year-long nightmare behind that formidable reserve of his.

'Not exactly a story calculated to put either of us in a party mood,' Duarte remarked broodingly.

'If you would like to put her pictures back up, you can,' Emily mumbled, that being the biggest sacrifice and apology she could conceive at that particular moment.

Duarte dealt her a look of sheer bewilderment.

'I feel sad for Izabel and you now. Poor Victorine too…all those pathetic tales she fed me about her perfect daughter and I can even understand why she did it now—'

'An alarming inability to deal with reality?' Duarte suggested.

'No, she wanted to remember Izabel as she might have been without the drug abuse—remember the good things, not the bad. Maybe you would feel better if you copied her a little…' Emily muttered awkwardly.

'There *were* no good things,' Duarte grated with sudden savage impatience. 'Why do you think I married you?'

'I'm not sure I want to know, in the mood you're in,' Emily said gently.

But Duarte was determined to tell her. 'After Izabel, I swore that no woman would ever have that kind of power over me again,' he breathed with stark bitterness.

Oh, well, that was really not news, Emily reflected, understanding that he was in an explosively emotional frame of mind after finally rising to the demeaning brink of admitting that his first marriage had been a disaster. Perhaps he might eventually reach the healthy point of wondering why his second marriage had run into rough waters as well.

For Emily could now see that *she* had paid the price for the amount of pain, humiliation and disillusionment that the self-destructive Izabel had inflicted on Duarte. Once bitten, forever shy. She also understood there was much that he'd *not* said, for she could read between the lines. He had really loved Izabel because he had not given up on her. How many times had he struggled to help Izabel and had his efforts thrown back in his face?

Somewhat put out by Emily's stoic and seemingly unresponsive silence, Duarte drove a not quite steady hand through his black luxuriant hair. Baulked of a further outlet, he said bossily, 'You should be getting ready for the party.'

And display body parts she much preferred to conceal beneath long skirts and sleeves and loose tops that hinted at more than she possessed. Like a lamb to the slaughter, she gathered up his gifts and went for a shower to freshen up.

When it crossed her mind that if she wore her hair down with that brief dress and low heels, she might look like she was mostly hair and vertically challenged, she decided to put her mane of red-gold hair up instead. Show off her neck. Why not? All else was going to be bared. Having donned the dress, an hour later, there was no temptation for her to examine her reflection in the mirror.

As she came downstairs she noticed that some gifted person had worked wonders with the floral disarrangement she'd abandoned earlier. Duarte strode out of one of the ground-floor reception rooms. Clad in a well-cut dinner jacket, he looked devastatingly male. Her heart skipped a beat but now there was a kernel of resentment.

Duarte focused on her with intent dark golden eyes and stilled as if someone had yanked an off switch inside him.

Emily started backing up the stairs again. 'I could have told you…I look like you don't feed me. Give me two minutes and I'll be covered up again!'

Duarte strode forward. 'You look breathtaking…'

Full marks for stunned stare of appreciation, she thought

and waited on the punchline that she was sure was about to come and then she would be a good sport and laugh.

'Gorgeous, *minha jóia*.'

Emily winced. 'No, I'm not.'

Duarte grabbed her hand and practically carried her over to the giant gilded mirror on the paneled wall. 'What do you see?'

'I'm not looking. I don't like my legs, my arms, my—er—other bits.'

'I love them,' Duarte husked bending over her. 'You have beautiful legs—'

'They're too short,' she hissed.

'Very shapely ankles, dainty arms, a neck like a swan's—'

'It's not long enough—'

'*Everything* in perfect proportion and you look distinctly ethereal in that shade of blue—'

'Spectral and gaunt?' She inched up her eyelashes.

'Ravishing. You grew up with two sisters jealous that you outshone them entirely in the looks department. Stop tormenting yourself with your non-existent flaws,' Duarte urged with a frank exasperation that had a much more powerful effect on her confidence than his compliments.

Finally studying her reflection, Emily saw herself as she had never seen herself. Elegant, slim and small it was true but not scrawny. Putting her hair up had been a good idea for now she could see that her face had a shape and her eyes looked all bright and starry. She turned ever so slightly sideways to check out the bosom profile. No improvement there but my goodness that dress flattered her, particularly the colour!

She looked in the mirror and met Duarte's intent gaze. He dealt her a hot, sizzling appraisal that spoke lustful volumes and made her quiver in helpless response. Well, she was ravishing him, anyway. 'My sisters aren't jealous of me—far from it,' she told him ruefully.

'Why else would they always be putting you down and cracking jokes at your expense?'

She sighed. 'It's just always been that way...their sense of humour, I suppose.'

'And your mother either acting as if it's not happening or even joining in. I know you care about your family but I think you need to assert yourself and make them treat you with respect.'

At that point the front doors were opened wide to greet the arrival of their first guests. There was no time for further conversation but she was disconcerted by what he'd said. It hurt that he had noticed her family's lack of respect but she was touched that he was concerned enough to advise her. Unfortunately, she could not imagine standing up to demand anything from her far more assertive elder sisters.

The party was in full swing by the time Bliss arrived and made an entrance. Every male head turned to watch Bliss glide across the room, her shapely figure enhanced by a scarlet silk sheath dress that was a far cry from her discreet business suits.

Her heartbeat accelerating, Emily watched Duarte cut through the crush to greet his executive assistant and she turned away again. There was *nothing* going on between Bliss and Duarte, she told herself firmly. They had become friends. She would just have to learn to live with that.

Duarte was not acting like a male involved in an affair. Duarte was behaving very much like a male who wanted to keep his marriage intact. She'd actually made it to that holy of holies once denied, a shared marital bed! He had told her about Izabel. He was entranced by their son. He had bought her a whole outfit and it did seem to do something special for her. Then there were the sapphires which had attracted many admiring comments and every time she said 'Duarte gave them to me,' she felt like a million dollars.

So she was looking on the bright side, refusing to dwell on murky suspicions for which she had no proof. Bliss Jarrett had always been a man's woman and very ambitious. It was hardly surprising that she should have ditched her covert friendship with Emily and chosen to shift her allegiance to Duarte instead. And, to be fair, Emily reflected ruefully, possibly Bliss *did* thoroughly dislike her now for what her foolish flight from Portugal had done to Duarte.

While she talked herself mentally into that state of calm and security, Emily drank her way through two glasses of wine. She rarely touched alcohol, for she did not have much of a head for it, but she felt in dire need of a little Dutch courage.

'Emily...?' called a bright familiar voice.

It was Bliss, all smiles and self-satisfaction. 'I've arranged a terrific party, haven't I?'

'Yes...absolutely.' Emily plastered what she hoped was a serene smile on to her lips and prayed for an interruption.

Across the room, she glimpsed Duarte, his brilliant eyes centred on both women. Emily smiled so hard at Bliss her face hurt.

'He's mine. Just you watch me in action,' Bliss invited.

'I trust him...' Emily didn't know if she did but it sounded good and strong. What she really wanted to do was lock Duarte up somewhere very secure, just to be on the safe side.

'When Duarte found you, he was about to instigate divorce proceedings.'

Emily widened her eyes in the desperate hope that that made her look incredulous. 'I asked for a divorce. He said no.'

'I don't believe that for a moment!' Bliss derided with

blistering scorn. 'We're lovers. Haven't you worked that out yet?'

Emily froze. Her heart divebombed to the soles of her feet. Her tummy performed a sickening somersault. 'I don't believe you.'

'Suit yourself.' Bliss simply laughed and walked away.

Emily finished her wine with a shaking hand. *Lovers!* That announcement was not a cue to panic, she instructed herself. In dismay, she watched Duarte move out on to the dance floor with Bliss. Emily wriggled through the clumps of chattering guests round the edge of the floor. Peering under arms for a better view and stretching her neck and standing on tip toe, she kept Duarte and Bliss under close surveillance.

She lifted another glass from a passing tray and watched Bliss press her lithe body into intimate connection with Duarte. But a moment later, Duarte backed off from that contact. Bad move, Bliss, he's not into intimate displays in front of audiences, Emily thought angrily. But then, when had Bliss ever been able to resist a challenge? Hadn't Bliss once told her that a clever woman could easily manipulate any man into doing her bidding? Now Bliss was whispering coyly into Duarte's ear. Duarte flung his arrogant head back and laughed and Emily felt stabbed to the heart and her bravado curdled at source.

If he fell for an Izabel, he could fall for a Bliss. *Lovers?* While she herself had been in England? Emily didn't know what to believe. One minute she was suffering agonies of jealousy but the next, she was telling herself that she could not trust anything that Bliss said. Forcing herself to stop spying on her husband and his 'friend', Emily turned on her heel.

Only minutes later, Duarte curved an imprisoning hand to her elbow and tugged her back against him to murmur ruefully, 'The one drawback of those shoes is that I can't see you in the crowd. Where have you been?'

'Oh...around.'

Now it seemed it was her turn to be whirled round the dance floor. She snuggled up so close to his lean hard body that a postcard could not have squeezed between them. Duarte tensed a little in surprise.

'If you push me away, you're *dead*,' Emily swore. 'It's bad enough having to smell *her* perfume on you.'

'Isn't jealousy hell?' Duarte imparted with a silken lack of concern that was just about the last reaction she had expected to receive.

'What would you know about it?' Emily snatched in a charged breath and then just stormed right to the heart of the matter. 'Bliss told me that you were lovers!'

Assailed by that dramatic contention, Duarte responded in the most withering of tones, '*Que absurdo!* Why would Bliss say such a thing? That is not my idea of a joke, Emily.'

'Are you saying you don't believe me?' Emily's voice rose in volume at the same velocity as her temper.

Duarte tightened the arm he had curved to her rigid spine like a restraining bar. 'No comment—'

'If you don't give me a straight answer, I'm walking off this floor!'

'You've been drinking...you're upset—'

Emily flung her head back and studied him with tormented aquamarine eyes. No. He didn't believe her. He was being smooth, evasive, possibly even extremely *cunning*.

'Bliss said that you weren't comfortable with her being here,' Duarte murmured very drily. 'Even at a distance of a hundred feet, I could see that too. You really don't need to make up childishly silly stories as well.'

Emily wrenched herself free of him with a sudden movement that took him by surprise. She felt violent, furious, incredibly bitter. Bliss and her games, always one step ahead. Duarte? If he was innocent, nothing short of a tape-recording would convince Duarte that Bliss had said such a thing. If he was guilty, all he had to do was accuse his wife of being intoxicated and jealous!

Concentrating on avoiding Duarte, Emily circulated. Every time he came within twenty feet of her, she moved on and plunged into animated conversation with someone else. At last their guests began to take their leave but it was a slow process. Then an elderly woman announced that her handbag had gone missing and immediately became very upset. Emily could have done with her husband's calming presence—her own level of Portuguese was unequal to the challenge of soothing the poor woman. Unfortunately, Duarte was nowhere within view and Emily had to martial the anxious and weary staff into an ordered search. The bag was finally found intact in the cloakroom. Telling the servants just to go to bed and clean up the party debris in the morning, Emily ushered their volubly apologetic guest out to her limousine with great relief.

As Emily walked back indoors, the big house felt eerily silent and empty. Had Duarte just gone up to bed? From the amount of light reflecting on the landing window, Emily realised that the lights had been left on outside in the court-yard garden. With a groan, she went back downstairs to switch them off. She frowned when she saw that the garden doors were still open and then she stopped dead in her tracks: Duarte and Bliss were outside.

Even as Emily looked, Bliss made a sudden almost compulsive movement and tipped forward into Duarte's swiftly extended arms. They were locked together like two magnets in the split second it took Emily to surge forward and gasp strickenly, 'You rotten, lying bastard!'

CHAPTER NINE

DUARTE thrust Bliss hurriedly back from him and wheeled round, his lean strong face startled, his whole demeanour one of almost exaggerated incredulity.

'Did you think I'd gone to bed?' Emily's voice broke on that rather meaningless demand but her brain was locked on that intimate image of them together and the sheer horror of the discovery that her very worst fears should have been proven right before her eyes.

Bliss strolled forward, her scarlet dress shimmering in the lights, her exquisite face offensively cool and collected. 'This is rather embarrassing but I do assure you that you misunderstood what you just saw. I simply stumbled and Duarte saved me from a nasty fall—'

'Do you honestly think I'm s-stupid enough to swallow that old chestnut?' Emily stammered, half an octave higher, utterly thrown by the blonde's reaction until she worked out that Bliss was assuming yet *another* role and this time for Duarte's benefit. That of supportive lover engaged in a tactful cover-up!

Duarte studied Emily's drawn and accusing face and he squared his broad shoulders. 'Don't be silly, Emily,' he urged in the most galling tone of authority. 'It's a warm night and Bliss was feeling faint. She almost fell and I steadied her. *End of story.*'

Duarte rested expectant dark deepset eyes on his wife.

Instantly, Emily looked away, away from both of them. She was trembling and sick with shock at their behaviour. Why were they doing this to her? Couldn't Duarte, at least, have come clean? Instead, they stood united against *her*, both of them making the same stupid excuse and both of them treating her as if she was an hysteric making wild childish allegations!

'I think I ought to go home, Duarte. I'm so sorry about this,' Bliss sighed with regret.

Enraged by the other woman's composure, Emily spun back. 'Tell me, what role are you playing now, Bliss? You're a very good liar but I have to admit that my head's spinning tonight!'

'Get a grip on yourself, Emily,' Duarte grated.

Emily couldn't bring herself to look at him. She kept on staring at Bliss. 'Have you told my husband about what a great friend you were to me before I left Portugal?'

'I really don't know what you're referring to,' Bliss responded drily.

'Oh, really?' Emily marvelled that she herself did not simply spontaneously combust with rage and sheer violent frustration. 'You mean you don't remember all those cosy lunches we shared at the Faz Figura restaurant in the Alfama? You don't recall the dozen shopping trips either? Not even my visits to your apartment?'

Bliss directed a marvellous look of sublime discomfiture at Duarte as if she was listening to the ravings of a very confused and drunken woman.

'Well then, if I never *visited* your apartment, tell me how I know that you have your dining room chairs covered in fake zebra skin?' Emily asked fiercely, determined to corner and entrap Bliss in her own lies. 'How come I know that you have a grandfather clock that belonged to your parents in your sitting room? Leather seats, glass tables—?'

As Emily's desperation to expose the blonde's lies rose to a charged peak, Bliss expelled a weary sigh. 'Well, I *do* have a leather suite but then so do many people and I would *adore* a grandfather clock but I've never owned one. As for the fake animal fur seats?' Bliss grimaced. 'I have rather better taste.'

Emily's rigid shoulders slumped. Evidently it would take someone a great deal cleverer than she was to catch Bliss out.

'Please go home, Bliss,' Duarte urged in an electrifyingly quiet request. 'I'm sorry you had to witness this.'

Bliss strolled past Emily like a queen and walked back indoors.

Duarte swore in driven Portuguese, and strode over to Emily, who was staring emptily into space. He gripped her by the arms to force her round to face him. 'What the hell has got into you? A friendship with Bliss? Since when? Are you paralytically drunk and delusional? How could you make such an ass of yourself?' he demanded with savage incredulity.

Emily was in a daze. 'Bliss *does* have a grandfather clock,' she protested shakily. 'And we were friends and I'm not drunk but I'm beginning to *feel* delusional!'

His smouldering dark golden eyes narrowed and he converted his hold on her limp arms to a supportive soothing hold. Looking distinctly at a loss, Duarte expelled his breath in a slow hiss. 'Look, I think you need to get some rest...OK?'

'You think I'm crazy. Or do you? Maybe you're as big a deceiver as *she* is! If that's how it is, fine. I don't care any more.' Emily raised her arms in an abrupt movement to shake free of his lean hands. Turning away from him, she set off down the corridor.

'I'll be upstairs in five minutes...' Duarte called after her. 'Do you want me to come up with you?'

'No, thanks.' If he thought she was going upstairs to share a bedroom with a male who thought she was only one mental step removed from a nervous breakdown, he had better think again.

Emily trudged back across the echoing main hall and out the front doors just in time to see the tail lights of Bliss's sleek silver sports car disappearing down the winding drive. Naturally one grandfather clock would now be speedily disposed of or possibly Bliss had got rid of that parental legacy months ago, Emily reflected numbly, for the clock had not suited the ultra-modern decor of Bliss's city apartment.

Unable to bear the claustrophobic silence of the house or the prospect of another confrontation with Duarte, Emily wandered out into the moonlit gardens. The dew-wet grass crunched beneath her feet. The palms cast spiky, mysterious shadows that faded the further she moved away from the house. She saw the domed bulk of the building the Monteiros called a summerhouse glimmering in the darkness beneath the trees. A grand eighteenth-century folly built of white marble, it was large enough to house a full orchestra. Mounting the steps, Emily dropped down on to a hard marble bench. Just then, the folly had a great deal more appeal than any bed containing Duarte.

Her husband thought she was nuts. He had gone from outraged disbelief to sudden grave concern. Right now, he was probably ringing one of his many medical friends to ask for some serious advice and book her an appointment with a psychiatrist.

In the quiet of the folly, Emily skimmed her shoes off to flex her crushed toes and willed herself to be calm. She saw that once again she had been set up by Bliss. Having seen Emily watching her with Duarte, Bliss had staged a pretend fall. No other explanation made sense. If Duarte wanted to snatch Bliss into a passionate embrace, he was highly unlikely to do so in a well-lit courtyard in full view of more than forty windows.

So, in that sense, she *had* made an ass of herself, Emily acknowledged grimly. But it was difficult to care when she was truly at the end of her tether. Bitterness was rising

inside her like a dam surging to break its banks. Assert
yourself, Duarte had told her when he was telling her how
to deal with her own family.

But when had she ever asserted herself with *Duarte*? She
was Mrs Doormat Monteiro and it was little wonder that
Bliss was able to best her at every turn. Eleven months ago,
Duarte had demanded a separation and he had dispatched
her to the house in the Douro and she had gone without a
murmur. She had behaved as if she *was* an unfaithful wife!

Why? She had been consumed with guilt over a kiss that
she had neither invited nor enjoyed. Why had she beaten
herself up for so long over that stupid episode? She had
not been unfaithful and she had not betrayed her husband.
But, totally intimidated by Duarte's chilling rage and his
even more appalling conviction that she had actually been
sleeping with Toby Jarrett, she had become so distraught
that she had been incapable of offering a convincing self-
defence.

As Emily sat there ruminating on her cold marble bench,
she began to see that she had spent most of the twenty-two
years of her life blaming herself for every bad and unlucky
thing that had ever happened to her. When her parents
didn't hug her as a child and her older sisters bullied her,
she had assumed that the fault was in her and not in them.
She had felt guilty and ashamed that she wasn't sufficiently
loveable and had just tried harder and harder to please in
the hope that somehow matters would improve. Only they
never had improved, she conceded sadly.

Then she had married Duarte. Duarte with his domi-
neering force of will and powerful personality. She had put
up with everything thrown at her. Victorine, Duarte's endless absences on business, a lifestyle she disliked. Had she
ever complained? No! She had blamed herself for not being
content with what she had and for wanting too much.

Instead of putting the blame squarely where it belonged on Duarte's shoulders.

Hearing a twig snap somewhere nearby, Emily froze into stillness.

'Are you trying to play hide-and-seek now?' Duarte derided as he strode into view from below the screening darkness of the trees. 'It is three o'clock in the morning. Do you realise how long I've been searching for you? How concerned I've been? If I hadn't found your tracks across the grass, I'd have been turning the staff out of bed to look for you!'

Emily studied him with a glorious sense of calm and not the smallest desire to apologise for her lack of consideration. In moonlight, Duarte was a dramatic study in black and white. So tall, so dark, so handsome. Always in control, preferably in control of *her*—yet he was losing his reserve at a staggeringly fast rate this time around. Why? She wasn't the same woman she had been at the time of their separation, eleven months ago.

'You really have been a lousy husband,' Emily sighed. 'And I don't need to be hysterical or intoxicated or nuts to tell you that—'

'You can abuse me all you like *indoors*,' Duarte stated icily. 'I refuse to stand around in the garden at this hour listening to this nonsense.'

'Fine. Goodnight,' Emily said quietly.

'Look, you're overwrought—'

'You're not at the bank, Duarte…so drop the command tone of voice. I won't be bullied or browbeaten—'

'But you might just be strangled,' Duarte intoned, mounting the steps at an aggressive pace. 'Now, I understand that you feel threatened by Bliss and that it may even be my fault that you feel jealous and insecure—but no way are you going to make a major event out of that stupid incident in the courtyard!'

'Am I not?' Emily sat up a little straighter and raised her chin.

'It's outright nonsense for you to pretend that you suspect me of infidelity!' Duarte delivered in the same thunderous tone. 'And, in your heart, you *know* it is—'

'Do I?' was all Emily said and not in a tone that suggested she was greatly interested in the subject.

'I would not have an affair with an employee—'

'I thought she was your friend...and wasn't I once an employee? And in a much humbler capacity than Bliss has ever been.'

Duarte dealt her an electrifying look of smouldering frustration. 'That was different!'

'So maybe Bliss was what you call different, too—'

'Are you *trying* to wind me up?' Duarte demanded incredulously, staring at her expressionless face with probing intensity.

'Why would I do that? Bliss need not be a problem, Duarte...providing that you can prove to my satisfaction that you are innocent.'

'What the hell is that supposed to mean?' he launched at her.

'That this evening I witnessed something suspicious between you and Bliss,' Emily reminded him in the same reasonable tone that seemed to be making his even white teeth clench. 'I don't need to justify my expectation that you should now immediately convince me beyond *all* reasonable doubt that you are blameless.'

'And how am I supposed to do that?' Duarte bit out furiously.

Emily lifted a slight shoulder and dropped it again. 'I don't know. It's not my problem, is it?'

'I've had enough of this!' Duarte growled and, taking a sudden step forward, he bent down and scooped her off the bench and up into his powerful arms. 'You've gone hay-

wire since last night! You're trying to play games with
me—'

'By demanding that you prove yourself innocent? Was
it a game when you did the same thing to me after seeing
Toby kiss me?' Emily asked dulcetly.

Duarte froze. 'So *that* is what this is all about...'

Imprisoned in his arms and as limp as a rag doll, Emily
looked up at him. 'And I've been much kinder to you than
you were to me in the same circumstances—'

'Just keep quiet or I'll lose my temper!' Duarte seethed,
arms tightening round her slight figure as he strode down
the steps and headed back towards the house.

'I mean, you can't say that I sat you down, stood over
you like a hanging judge and frightened you to the extent
that you just fell apart at the seams...can you?'

'Shut up!' he roared.

'You see, I'm not a bully—'

'What did you say?'

'I think you heard me—'

'*Inferno!* I am bloody well not a bully!' Duarte raged,
jawline rockhard. 'How dare you accuse me of being a
bully?'

'Well, if carting me back indoors without my consent is
not bullying, I don't know what is.'

Duarte jerked to a very abrupt halt. 'I'm looking after
you, not bullying you,' he framed, in such a rage he could
hardly get the words out.

'But I don't want to be looked after. I can look after
myself and I can walk on my own legs.'

With hugely exaggerated care, Duarte lowered her to the
grass. Only then did she realise that her shoes had been left
behind in the folly. Duarte had been well aware of the fact.
He gave her a sardonic smile.

'Thanks,' she said compressing her lips.

'That night I saw you in Jarrett's arms, I controlled my

temper. How many men would have done that?' Duarte demanded rawly.

'I was very upset and I felt guilty even though I hadn't done anything and you scared me—'

'I didn't lay a finger on you!' Duarte bit out.

'No,' Emily agreed unevenly. 'But I was scared that you might—'

'When have I *ever* hurt you?' His bronzed features very pale in the light still cascading from the *quinta*, Duarte stared at her in fierce reproach.

'Never. But that night I was scared—and, because I was scared and very upset, I made a hash of explaining myself to you. You didn't listen anyway. You were already convinced that I had betrayed you. Yet what did you see?' she prompted tautly. 'You saw him grab me and kiss me—'

'I was around long before that,' Duarte cut in grimly. 'I heard him begging you to run away with him and a whole hell of a lot of other juvenile rubbish!'

'Until Toby spoke, I had no idea that he believed that he was in love with me. I was in shock and I didn't want to hurt him and I didn't know what to say—'

'So you just stood there and let him kiss you. If that's as good as your story gets, don't waste your breath trying to raise the subject again!'

'Well, I'm looking forward to seeing how you plan to convince me that you have been one hundred per cent faithful to me for the whole of our marriage,' Emily countered in a slightly strained voice as she picked her way painfully across the gravel fronting the house in her bare feet.

'I expect you to trust me' Duarte informed her without the smallest hesitation.

'I expected you to trust me and look where it got me,' Emily countered without hesitation. 'So please don't expect me to be more generous than you were.'

On the steps of the house, she stopped to brush off the

gravel embedded in the stinging soles of her feet. That task achieved, she headed straight for the sweeping staircase.

'Emily…this is ridiculous,' Duarte breathed wearily. 'When you vanished for eight months, I thought it would serve you right if I did find another woman but I didn't *do* it!'

'Prove it,' she said without turning her head.

'How the hell can I *prove* it?' he raked at her rigid back. 'Call in character witnesses?'

Emily was so exhausted after the effort it had taken to stand up to Duarte's towering personality, she was beyond any further thought or action. In any case, since she had long since sent the staff to bed, Duarte was going to have to douse lights and lock up, which was likely to take him quite a while. In the bedroom that she'd never shared with him before, she dug her teddy nightshirt out from under the bed, padded into the bathroom and stripped where she stood. Donning the nightshirt, she freshened up and pulled the clips out of her piled-up hair, letting it fall round her in a wild tangle. On her passage to the bed, she remembered the sapphires she still wore. Setting the earrings and the necklace down on the cabinet, she slid between the sheets and lay there, barely able to keep her heavy eyes open.

Had she got anywhere with Duarte? Had he seen the point that she'd been trying to make? That he had judged *her* on superficial evidence? Where had his trust been? Had he ever trusted her? It was not as if she'd ever been a femme fatale, who flirted like mad with other men and gave him cause for concern.

Duarte strode into the bedroom like a threatening storm ready to rain down thunder and lightning. As his attention settled on the slight bump she made in his bed, some of his high-voltage tension visibly ebbed.

Emily sighed, tucked her hand under the pillow and

turned on her side to go to sleep. 'G'night,' she mumbled sleepily.

'Right...so now I'm getting the big freeze!'

She thought about that and sighed again. 'I'm just tired.'

Ten minutes later, he tugged her across the bed into his arms and she groaned out loud while surreptitiously snuggling back into the hard heat of him. He turned her round to face him, brilliant dark golden eyes still ablaze with vibrant energy.

'Bliss *did* have a grandfather clock,' he murmured with the air of a male expecting a burst of applause. 'And no, I have never been in her apartment but I do recall her telling me a long time ago that the only thing her father left her when he died was an ugly big clock. An appraiser had advised her to keep it as an investment and she had it shipped out here.'

'Congratulations,' Emily mumbled, eyes dropping closed again.

'You can't go to sleep now, *minha jóia*,' Duarte ground out incredulously. 'Did you hear what I said?'

'Talk about it in the morning—'

'It *is* the morning and we're flying over to London in precisely six hours' time,' Duarte reminded her with considerable impatience and he shook her shoulder slightly, lifted and dropped her limp hand, striving to rouse her again.

But nothing short of a fire alarm would have wakened Emily or persuaded her to take the slightest interest in anything other than sleep.

'Anyone ever tell you that you sleep like the dead?'

'You.' Glancing up from the magazine she was pretending to read, Emily noted anxiously that once again, Duarte was staring at her from his seat opposite. He had been doing that ever since she came down to breakfast two hours earlier and yet he had barely spoken to her. The drive to the airport had been similarly filled with unspoken tension and in half an hour the jet would be landing in London.

'Tell me, do you remember what I said to you last night just before you feel asleep?' Duarte enquired with studied casualness.

Emily chewed at her lower lip and silently shook her head. It was a lie. She did have a vague recollection of him accusing her of giving him the big freeze but that was not a subject she was particularly keen to reopen, for she was all too well aware that when she had wakened around seven in his arms she had *not* given him the big freeze. Reddening at that mortifying awareness of her own drastic lack of control, Emily returned to her fake perusal of the magazine and wondered why she'd dreamt about Bliss's grandfather clock during the night. Quite where and how the clock had figured in her dream, she could not recall.

'You're just so quiet,' Duarte remarked.

'Last night drained me,' she muttered honestly.

'You made your point. You more than made your point,' Duarte extended. 'But I assure you that I have *never* been intimate with Bliss Jarrett.'

Emily nodded, much as if she was listening to a weather report.

'At least *look* at me...' Duarte intoned in low-pitched frustration, evidently as aware as she was of the presence of the nanny nursing Jamie at the other end of the cabin.

Slowly Emily raised her head, aquamarine eyes full of strain.

She encountered stunning dark golden eyes that made her own instantly sting with tears and hurriedly she dropped her head again.

'Please don't cry...' Duarte leant forward and grasped her knotted fingers between both his hands. 'I feel enough of a bastard as it is.'

Emily gulped.

'I've really screwed up our marriage,' Duarte muttered half under his breath, startling her into looking up again—but there was nothing to be gained but a view of Duarte's gleaming dark springy hair bent over their linked hands. 'I don't want you to argue with me about that.'

Emily surveyed his bent head in growing wonderment. She had no intention whatsoever of arguing with him on that score. There was a moment of awkward silence while he gave her a chance to argue in his defence. His wide shoulders emanated ferocious tension when the silence remained unbroken.

'In the future I will do a lot of things differently,' Duarte swore, practically crushing the life out of her fingers, every word emerging stilted and raw with emotion. 'I'm not the most liberated guy around but I can change. Ordering people around just comes very naturally to me...'

'I know,' Emily whispered. 'It's just I'm not really sure why you're talking like this—'

Duarte lifted his proud head and his incisive dark golden eyes glittered over the bemused expression on her face. 'I didn't sleep last night. I kept on getting flashbacks of you cowering in a chair in front of me after I caught...*saw*,' he adjusted hastily, 'you in Toby Jarrett's arms that night. I don't think you got out a single sentence that I didn't interrupt—'

'I didn't—but maybe I was a bit tough on you last night because understandably, you were very, very angry with me after what you saw—'

'Emily, shut up,' Duarte groaned. 'You probably weren't tough enough. I need you to stand up to me—'

'I don't like confrontations but I'll try.' Emily watched Duarte breathe in very deep and slow. 'You don't need to say anything more. I know why you're saying all these things...'

'You *do*?' Duarte looked dubious.

'You're afraid that I'm planning to get off this plane and take Jamie and refuse ever to come back to Portugal but I wouldn't *do* that to you again,' Emily assured him heavily.

'Actually…' Duarte released her hand and flung himself back into his own seat. He surveyed her with bleak dark eyes. 'That *wasn't* why I was saying those things. For once in my life, you are ahead of me. Believe it or not, I hadn't considered that possibility.'

'I won't part you from Jamie,' Emily reaffirmed a second time.

'If you come back to Portugal with me this evening, you can have the dress, the honeymoon and the very moon itself if you ask for it,' Duarte asserted with brooding darkness. 'Whatever you choose to do, I will not issue any threats.'

Emily was hurt that he had so little faith in her promises. She just could not fathom what was going on inside that darkly handsome head of his. He was like a man suffering from ever-growing shock. His moods were all over the place. He was as tense as a rumbling volcano. He was talking like she had never heard him talk before in his life. Was he really so scared of losing Jamie? Then why wouldn't he be? Without very much thought at all, she had denied him any contact with his son for many months. How could she blame him for doubting her?

'Duarte…there's a couple of things I'd like to say,' Emily admitted in a rush. 'Please listen, even though you don't believe what I'm telling you…'

'I'm listening…'

'I never told you that I had become friendly with Bliss because she said that you'd think it was inappropriate and that it might damage her career prospects with you,' Emily related, deliberately not looking at him lest she lose her nerve. 'I met Toby in her apartment and she persuaded me to let him paint me. The portrait was supposed to be a present for you—'

'I don't really want to hear any more,' Duarte incised in a charged undertone.

Emily ignored him and started talking even faster so that she could finish. 'When I left the house in the Douro eight months ago, it was only because Bliss phoned me to warn me that she had overheard *you* speaking to your lawyer and discussing your chances of taking my baby away from me as soon as he was born.'

The silence simmered like a heatwave about to explode into violence.

Emily mustered her courage and glanced at Duarte. His attention carefully pinned to some point in the middle distance, his bronzed skin was stretched super-taut across his hard bone structure. Pallor was stamped round his set mouth, the pallor a male restraining and containing rage.

'Is there any more?' he almost whispered.

'Nothing important.' Shrivelled by his silent, smouldering reaction to her revelations, Emily grabbed up her magazine again, grateful the jet was coming in to land.

Thirty minutes later, in the crowded concourse inside the airport, Emily turned to say to Duarte, 'I'm leaving Jamie with you...OK?'

Her husband emerged from his extreme preoccupation and frowned at her. 'But we're going to see your family together—'

'I thought you had a business meeting—'

'I had it rescheduled.'

Emily interpreted that sudden announcement as confirmation that he did not trust even *her* out of his sight, never mind Jamie. 'It's just I'd prefer to see my family alone—'

'I'm coming with you,' Duarte informed her in a studiously level tone. 'We'll let Jamie and his nanny go straight to Ash Manor and join them there later.'

'You're not listening to me. I want to speak to my mother alone. I want to talk to her in private. I don't want company.'

'When I said I could make changes, I did not mean I could turn into New Age man overnight,' Duarte drawled. 'Your mother will walk all over you and upset you. She always does. If I'm there she stays within certain limits.'

'I don't want New Age man, Duarte...I just want you to respect my wishes.'

'Don't say you weren't warned, *minha esposa*.'

Odd how he could boss her about with such sublime cool himself but react like a caged lion at the mere prospect of anyone else taking advantage of her easy-going nature. It was a kind of territorial possessiveness, she supposed vaguely. Feeling sympathetic, she allowed him to arrange for a limo to take her to her family home when she could perfectly well have climbed on the train and got there much faster.

CHAPTER TEN

'I SUPPOSE you had better come in,' Lorene Davies said grudgingly when she found her daughter on the doorstep of her smart detached home.

Nervous as a cat, Emily watched her mother's slim, straight back disappear into the kitchen. An attractive blonde woman well into her fifties, she looked a good decade younger. Following her disinterested parent, Emily hovered in the kitchen doorway while Lorene continued to stack her dishwasher with plates. Not much of a welcome after her eight-month absence, Emily thought tautly. But then, had she really expected anything different?

'Been in touch with your husband recently?' the older woman asked with her first flicker of curiosity. 'He came here looking for you last year and he seemed to blame us for not keeping you here. It was really very embarrassing and, I can tell you, I was very annoyed about it. You've always been a problem, Emily.'

Emily stiffened, thinking she'd been the quietest, tidiest and most helpful child in the household but had only ever earnt criticism in return for her best efforts.

'Look, I'm sure you don't want me taking up your time when you're so busy. I won't keep you long,' Emily murmured, her nails digging into the palms of her clenched hands as she willed herself on. 'I'm only here for one reason. I hope you can give me an honest answer and I promise not to hold it against you—'

'What on earth are you rambling on about?' Lorene Davies demanded angrily, unaccustomed to her timid daughter addressing her in such a manner. Emily forced her chin up and stood as tall as she could. 'I have a right to know why you don't like me—'

'Don't be ridiculous! Don't like you? What's that supposed to mean?' Her mother said scornfully. 'You have such odd ways, Emily.'

Emily lost what little colour she had. 'If I'm odd, you made me odd. I need to hear a reason from you and then I'll leave you in peace.'

Tight-mouthed, Lorene studied her for a long timeless moment of tension. 'All right. Before we moved up here from Cornwall, I had an affair and lived with another man for a while. That man was your *real* father...'

'What are you telling me?' Emily mumbled, her skin coming up in gooseflesh.

'What you said you wanted to know.' Lorene folded her arms, looking defiant and bitter. 'His name was Daniel Stevenson. He owned a big stud farm. Daniel said he was going to marry me when my divorce came through but he changed his mind when I was about seven months pregnant. He told me to go back to my husband and he slung us out—'

'My father—Peter Davies *isn't*...my father?' Emily said sickly.

'No, but when I went back to Peter he said he'd raise you as his child and we moved up here to make a fresh start. That's more or less it.'

'This Daniel Stevenson...I look like him, don't I?' Emily prompted chokily.

'You're the image of him,' Lorene confirmed grimly. 'He died about fifteen years ago. A riding accident. I can't say that I grieved when I heard about it. He was a creep. I really loved him but I was only one in a long line of foolish women—'

'I'm sorry...' Emily saw the core of her mother's hardness in the bitterness in her eyes. Lorene had been hurt, humiliated and abandoned.

'I'm sorry too,' the older woman muttered wearily. 'But I could never feel for you what I felt for your sisters. It wasn't your fault but I still can't look at you without remembering Daniel and I couldn't forgive him for what he did to me.'

'I can imagine. Thank you for finally telling me,' Emily managed to say and then she turned on her heel and walked straight back out of her childhood home. Her sisters had probably known the truth for years, she thought strickenly, possibly even recalling something of that time when their mother had taken them to live with Daniel Stevenson. Why had she been excluded from the secret?

For an instant she hovered on the outside step, struggling to get a hold on the shock consuming her. Duarte, where are you when I need you? The craving for Duarte was so strong she could've cried. Was she really going to tell him that sad little story? The unfaithful wife and the womaniser? Duarte with his incredibly respectable family tree and aristocratic background?

The front door behind her opened again. 'Would you like to come back in?' Lorene asked awkwardly.

'Thanks for the offer but no,' Emily muttered in harried surprise and without looking back she hurried back out to the limousine parked and screened by the high hedge.

Hurried steps sounded behind her. A hand briefly touched her arm. 'Emily, I'm sorry...' Lorene Davies suddenly sobbed.

In any other mood, Emily would have been astonished by that display of emotion in her direction but just then she could not deal with it and all she wanted was to escape. As she flew through the garden gate and back on to the pavement, the rear passenger door of the limousine opened and Duarte stepped fluidly out in front of her.

'What are you doing here?' she gasped chokily.

He scanned her pasty, white face and opened his arms and she threw herself against him with a strangled sob. She'd never been so glad to see anybody. It felt so good to be held. Nothing else seemed to matter. Nothing seemed to hurt so much. He lowered her into the car and nudged her along the seat to climb in beside her.

'How did you g-get here?' she stammered in bewilderment.

'Cab. I suspected that you were planning to confront your mother and I thought I should be within reach just in case it didn't pan out the way you wanted it to.'

She wiped her streaming eyes with the tissue he supplied. 'It didn't. I asked her why she didn't like me and I thought...I thought maybe she would deny it. Or say I had been an extra child she'd never wanted 'cos my sisters are so much older...or that I was a bad pregnancy or a very difficult baby—'

As the limo moved off, Duarte pulled her back against him and curved his arms lightly round her. 'And instead?'

'It turned out I'm the family's dirty secret—'

'Stop exaggerating,' Duarte urged, smoothing her tousled hair back from her damp brow. 'Come on...'

'Mum had an affair with a real creep and he was my father—'

'I suspected something of that nature,' Duarte confided quietly.

Emily tensed and tipped her head up to squint up at him in the most awkward way. 'You...*suspected*?'

'You don't resemble any one of your relatives, *minha jóia*. That in itself could have been simple genetics but, taken in tandem with the manner in which they treated you, it did make me wonder.'

Looked at from upside down, Duarte really did have the most incredible long lashes, Emily conceded absently. She sighed. 'I feel like I've just lost my whole life…like I'm not the person I thought I was—'

'You're Emily Monteiro,' Duarte reminded her instantaneously. 'We'll do some research on your true father if you like. A few details that did not relate to him being a "real creep" might help you come to terms with this.'

'My mother got so upset after telling me…but when she started telling me she was so hard about it.'

'She's probably been dying to get it off her chest for years but I'm sure she didn't get much of a kick out of confessing when it came to the point. Especially as, knowing you, you probably said thanks in your politest voice before tottering away.'

'Pretty much… How do you know that?'

'If you could thank me after I demanded a separation, you could certainly thank your mother for hurting you.'

Emily was so shaken by that statement that she pulled away from him and turned round to face him levelly. 'Did I say thanks that night after you had said you wanted a separation?'

Duarte nodded in confirmation. 'I took it to mean that you had decided that you *did* want to be with Toby Jarrett—'

'Oh, no…you misunderstood!' Aquamarine eyes aghast, Emily shook her head. 'How could you think that?'

'Emily…what I saw and heard that night was a major, not minor shock to my system and you weren't the only one of us saying things you hadn't thought through.'

'Oh… What did you want me to say?'

Duarte gave her an almost wry smile that tugged at her heartstrings for a reason she could not define. 'You were supposed to get down on bended knees and plead for a second chance. Instead you went upstairs and started packing.'

Emily shut her eyes and slumped back against the seat.

Duarte had just told her something she would rather not have known, for it tore her apart. She might have got all that nonsense about Toby cleared up there and then and they might never have separated at all!

'Why is it that you *seem* to be such a predictable woman and yet you never ever give me the response I expect?' Duarte demanded in rampant frustration.

'Sorry…'

'Forget it. I'll go back to my bad old ways. Easy as falling off a log,' Duarte assured her smooth as silk. 'We're going to embark on our honeymoon at Ash Manor. Agreed, it's *not* the Caribbean but the Caribbean does not have good associations for me—'

Duarte had her attention now. 'Honeymoon?' she parrotted.

'Bliss and Toby are off the conversational agenda for the moment,' Duarte decreed, warming visibly to the bad old ways of command.

'How can they be?'

'I'm logical, *minha jóia*. No controversial discussions equals no arguments. We can have a church blessing in Portugal and you can trot down the aisle in a rainbow of clashing colours—'

Emily fumbled to find her voice. 'Are you sending me up with all this?'

'Trying to take your mind off your newly discovered family connections.'

'You don't need to go that far—'

Duarte quirked a sardonic black brow. 'I admit that giving you the moon, if you ask for it, is likely to prove a problem—'

'But why…why would you do all this for me?'

'I want to stay married, *querida*. Much as I would like to, I can't chain you to the marital bed or force you to live with me. Basically, I'm endeavouring to launch a rescue bid on our marriage.' Duarte rested his spectacular dark eyes on her shuttered and still tear-stained face. 'If, at any point, you feel moved to offer even an ounce of enthusiasm for that venture, feel free to speak up.'

Emily tore her gaze from the undeniable enchantment of his and thought of how much she loved him, even when he was being unspeakably smart at her expense. 'This is all about Jamie…can't you just admit that?'

Duarte settled himself fluidly back into the far corner of the limo and scorched her with his golden eyes in challenge. 'Is that what you want?'

'Yes!'

'OK…it's about Jamie. I won't tax your patience with all the pros and cons of a child having two parents.'

Given the honesty she had believed she craved, Emily felt dreadful. He was willing to do *anything* to keep their marriage afloat for Jamie's benefit. 'I appreciate your honesty,' she said woodenly.

'Happy now?' Duarte prompted with what she considered to be sheer cruelty.

'Ecstatic…' she mumbled.

It was so strange to be back at Ash Manor as Duarte's wife. Those few days after their wedding, two years earlier, she'd still not felt like his wife. Duarte disappeared into the library to make some phone calls and she went off in search of Jamie. He greeted her with a little shout of pleasure and held out his arms to be lifted.

'Because you're a Monteiro, I'm going to stay one too,' she told her son mournfully but she could not stay down for long in his company.

Duarte loved his son. Duarte had experienced instant love and acceptance where his child was concerned. What did she get in comparison? She got the name, the wealth and now she was going to have the stupid dress and the stupid honeymoon rammed down her throat, whether she wanted them or not! On the other hand, whatever else Duarte was doing, he was not pining for Bliss, was he?

Why did she always want what she couldn't have? Duarte valued their marriage and that should be enough for her now. She'd grown up a lot—she'd stopped living in cloud cuckoo and hoping he might suddenly fall passionately in love with her. But at the same time, she should also be making demands. He was never likely to be more approachable or more willing to listen to her again.

She took Jamie out for a walk in his pram. It was a high coach affair purchased in Lisbon and totally impractical for country conditions. But while she bounced the pram down a grassy laneway beneath the trees, she was considering the demands she felt she ought to make. Having returned to the house and passed her sleeping son over to his nanny, she went into the drawing room and found writing paper and a pen. Then she wrote and she wrote and she wrote.

Duarte was still on the phone when she entered the library. He gave her a slow smile, brilliant eyes roaming over her tense pink face, skimming lower, lingering in provocative places as though he was touching her. He filled her with an awareness that was so strong she was embarrassed by her own susceptibility.

'I want you...' he murmured huskily as he tossed the phone aside and reached for her.

'I think you should read this first...' Emily slid her demand sheets across the polished surface of his desk.

'What's this, *minha jóia*?'

'My blueprint for the rescue bid,' she told him tautly.

Duarte laughed with vibrant amusement, tugged her down on to his lap and started to read. Then he gently and firmly lifted her off him again. 'I work no more than eight hours a day, the only exception being an emergency? That's not possible—'

'You could try it.'

'If I go abroad, you come too?'

'You could try going less often—'

'"For every day you spend away from me, I will spend a day away from you,"' Duarte read out loud in disbelief. 'That's blackmail. We would never see each other!'

'I need a life too—'

'*Do homemes a praça, da mulheres a casa,*' Duarte quoted that well-known Portuguese proverb with gravity. Men out and about, women at home.

'The rescue bid is off—'

He paled. 'OK. You win but have you ever heard of the art of compromise?'

'I did nothing but compromise the first time around and I was miserable and lonely.'

Looking grim, Duarte made it on to the second sheet and then he smiled at her with that sudden flashing charisma that could make her heart sing. 'Truthfully—you don't really want me out of your sight for longer than eight hours at a time?'

'If you want to think that, that's fine by me.'

His smile vanished. He skimmed through all the minor requests, even chuckled a few times and then, without any warning, he suddenly slung the last sheet aside and sprang upright. 'You don't want any more children with me? What kind of a condition is that?'

He looked so hurt, so full of reproach and incomprehension.

'You made me feel that I had to give you a baby when we first married and the truth is, I felt too young and I wasn't ready to be a mother then,' Emily admitted awkwardly.

'I never ever demanded that you give me a baby—'

'No but you took if for granted that I would.'

'If that is how you feel...didn't you *want* him?' Duarte shot at her in sudden emotive appeal.

'I adore Jamie but if ever I have another baby, it has to be because *I* want another baby.'

'All I can say is that I believed you felt the same way as me about having a family…'

She saw the sincerity in his eyes as he made that claim and felt terrible.

'Obviously I won't make the same mistake again,' Duarte drawled flatly. 'No wonder you were so miserable when you were pregnant—'

Emily's eyes shimmered. 'I was unhappy because after I became pregnant you just…well, I mean, you never touched me again—'

'Did you expect me to disregard the doctor's advice?' Duarte demanded in astonishment.

'What advice?' Emily frowned.

'Emily, you were present when the doctor advised us to desist from marital relations for the first few months!'

'I never heard him say that…' She sank down in the chair behind her. Thinking back, she remembered that during the first antenatal examination she had had, she had refused to have Duarte present and the nurse had translated the doctor's comments because the older man had not spoken English. When Duarte had been called back in the nurse had gone out and the doctor had talked at length to them both, but Emily hadn't paid much heed for she had trusted Duarte to translate anything of any further importance.

'You honestly didn't know?' Duarte raked an impatient hand through his black hair and stared at her. 'If you didn't understand, why didn't you ask me to explain afterwards, if not at the time?'

'I couldn't wait to get out of there! The whole time the doctor was examining me he was telling me off for being so thin and underweight and he was upsetting me. You never even mentioned it to me,' she condemned in turn.

'What was there to mention? Who wants to discuss a blanket ban on sex?'

'I misjudged you. I'm sorry. I wouldn't have locked the bedroom door if I'd known we were supposed to be de-sisting, or whatever he called it,' she lamented, feeling fool-ish. 'I felt so rejected.'

'I wasn't exactly celebrating either.' Reaching down, Duarte tugged her upright, his lean, strong face taut. 'We were like strangers when we first got married. I believed I could take a wife and that we could be content without being very close—'

'You chose the wrong woman—'

'I deserved a gold-digger.' He gazed down at her with rueful, dark-as-midnight eyes. 'I made you very unhappy.'

'I need closeness...'

'I'm working on it—but I'm really good at the physical end of the scale...' Duarte cupped her cheekbones, spread his fingers and drew her mouth under his with a hot, hungry urgency that nonetheless contained a vein of tenderness she had never felt from him before.

And suddenly she was kissing him back with the most desperate surging need powering through her, her slim body quivering at every contact with his. Breathing raggedly, he lifted his head. 'Let's go to bed—'

'It's barely tea time—'

'Let's go to bed—'

'What about Jamie's bath?'

'Our son has a nanny, and I can't wait and neither can you,' Duarte assured her with mesmeric intensity, shifting against her to acquaint her with his bold arousal, cupping her hips in the same sinfully erotic way to pull her up to him.

They got to the bedroom without meeting anyone, which had been Emily's only fear. Duarte brought her down on the bed fully clothed and came down on top of her and kissed her breathless. The need in her was so intense she was raw with it, shaken by her own desire. She just wanted him so much and his passion more than matched hers. He was wild for her and the more she recognised that, the more she threw off her inhibitions. She raked her nails down his back at the height of fulfilment and looked in stricken dismay at the marks she had left on his beautiful back in the aftermath.

Duarte just laughed and hugged her to him with easy strength. 'You just used me, *minha esposa*. As a vent for a very upsetting day. I'm not complaining but if I ever call back home at lunchtime and grab you off your feet and pin you flat to the nearest horizontal surface, you have to promise to be equally understanding.'

As Emily could not picture him dragging himself from the bank at lunchtime, she just pressed a kiss to a muscular brown shoulder and drifted off to sleep, satiated and secure.

CHAPTER ELEVEN

EMILY spun slowly round in front of the cheval mirror, admiring herself from every angle.

It was the wedding dress of her dreams. Romantic, filmy, the colour of champagne and the most superb fit. Her tiny waist was accentuated which had the miraculous effect of lending her the illusion of a fuller swell in the bosom department. Not that it mattered to anyone but her, for Duarte seemed to have a genuine passion for her just as she was.

Humming under her breath, she feasted her eyes upon herself. He would love the dress. She knew he was bracing himself for the clashing rainbow of colours because he was not to know that dear Bliss had convinced her that that was what most flattered her. But it had only taken one glimpse of herself clad in palest blue for Emily to see the light.

They had spent three weeks at Ash Manor, returning to Portugal only the night before. Three of the happiest weeks of her life. There was a kind of magic in the air between them. No doubt that was her romanticising his erotic and intense absorption in making love to her at every possible opportunity but they had had a lot of fun out of bed too. With Jamie. Out riding together. And all the time she'd been learning that she had spent a long time married to and living with a male she had never really got to know. But then, Duarte had not really wanted her to get to know him then.

'I thought you would be the kind of wife whom I would always find in the stables with the horses,' he had confided only the week before. 'Instead you were always out socialising and shopping and, when you were at home, you threw constant dinner parties. It reminded me of life with Izabel. I hated it.'

Instead of pleasing him with her efforts to fit the role she had assumed he wanted her to occupy, she had actually been pushing him away. The more she discovered, the more she loved him for what he was really telling her was that they were much better matched than she could ever have believed. He liked to entertain friends and family at home but he very much preferred to keep business connections out of their home.

He gave her flowers every day and laughed at the way her arrangements turned out. He gave her true affection that did not always lead to passion. He gave her everything but his heart. And she had pretty much given up on his heart. As she finally came to understand just how much Izabel had hurt him, she knew why he had had the reserve and that desire to control. His heart had brick walls round it except where Jamie was concerned and if she ever told him that all that was wrong with him was his gigantic unconfessed fear of being hurt again, he would never, ever forgive her.

After all, she'd already hurt him with Toby, hadn't she? She had dwindled into a poor little victim instead of forcing him to recognise that she was telling the truth.

As for Bliss, well, Emily believed that she'd already worked out the most likely scenario on that score. Duarte was probably going to admit to her that he had slept with Bliss during the difficult months that he had been searching for his wife and child. She was going to have to deal with that and she didn't know how she would. But that explanation made sense as to why Duarte should have insisted on not talking about Bliss for a few weeks, didn't it? Duarte had decided that if he had risked telling her the truth first, their marriage had no hope of surviving.

An impatient knock sounded on the door. 'Emily...?'

She smiled, suppressing the pained regret roused by her most recent thoughts. She opened the door a chink. 'Close your eyes...'

'No. I want to see you,' Duarte overruled. 'I've waited long enough.'

She opened the door wide and let him look.

His brilliant eyes shimmered over her. 'You look amazing. I was a selfish bastard two years ago—'

'I don't think you meant to be,' Emily told him forgivingly.

'That's right, Emily. Encourage me to be like that again.'

'What time do we have to be at the church for the blessing?' she prompted.

'We've got plenty of time—'

'Why won't you tell me what time?'

'I have a couple of people waiting downstairs and we need to deal with them first.' Duarte banded an arm to her spine as they reached the first landing.

'What people?'

'Had I had the option, I would've staged this weeks ago but I couldn't track the guy down. He was hiking round South America.'

'Who are you talking about?' Emily frowned.

Dropping his hand to her waist, Duarte ushered her towards the salon. 'Toby Jarrett.'

'*Toby?*' Emily gasped in pure horror. 'I don't want to see *him* again!'

However, a bigger shock awaited her within the salon. Not Toby, whom she was expecting, but Bliss. Bliss turned from the window with a saccharine smile that froze when she registered in visible bewilderment that Emily was wearing a wedding dress.

'We won't keep you long, Bliss,' Duarte drawled. 'To save us all a long trawl through murky waters, you could just confess to being a scheming, vindictive woman.'

Bliss blinked and stared at Duarte. 'I beg your pardon?'

'You weaseled your way into a fake friendship with my wife so that you could cause trouble. You never ever told me when Emily called the office and tried to speak to me. You also forgot to fill in my diary for the dinner parties—'

'I don't believe I'm hearing these terrible accusations,' Bliss said in a mortified tone of reproach.

Emerging from her own shock that Duarte should even have made such very accurate accusations, Emily's head turned as the door that connected with the dining room pushed open and framed Toby Jarrett. Emily's face reddened fiercely. Tall and fair and lanky, Toby moved deeper into the room.

'What are you doing here?' Bliss demanded sharply.

'I'm here to call your bluff,' Toby sighed, his frank open features grim. 'You offered me several thousand pounds to try and seduce Duarte's wife last year. I was broke but even I wasn't that low. I was quite happy to settle for the portrait commission—'

'He's telling outright lies!' Bliss snapped. 'Surely you don't believe this rubbish, Duarte?'

'Why *should* Toby lie?' Emily murmured tightly, focusing on the blonde with shaken eyes of revulsion after what the younger man had revealed. 'What has he got to gain from lying now?'

Duarte studied his executive assistant with chilling cool. 'I cannot blame Emily for trusting you when I made the mistake. You're sacked, Bliss—and, by the way, if you keep on telling people that I slept with you, I will take you to court for slander—'

'And how are you ever going to prove that you *didn't*?' Bliss slammed back at him and she gave Emily a cold look of triumph. 'You're never going to know for sure, are you?'

'I think the fact that you pulled the same stunt with your

last employer would go a long way to vindicating me,'
Duarte remarked very quietly.

Stilling at that response, Bliss turned white and then she
stared at her cousin in furious condemnation. *'Toby?'*

'Sorry—but when you came out to Lisbon to work on
the strength of a fake reference issued by one of my father's
friends, you promised that you were making a fresh start.'

'You did something like this *before*?' Emily demanded
of Bliss.

'Her last boss was married, too. She told a couple of
people in confidence that they were lovers and got the ru-
mour mill going,' Toby explained ruefully. 'Then she tried
to blackmail him by threatening to lie to his wife as well.
But he went to the police. Bliss got off with a police caution
but only because she managed to convince a doctor that
she had had a nervous breakdown.'

'Were you planning to blackmail Duarte too?' Emily
asked the blonde in horror.

Bliss seemed oddly diminished in stature but her eyes
were as hard as ever. Without troubling to respond—indeed, accepting that her every malicious act had been exposed—she just walked out of the room.

'I think she was hoping to *marry* Duarte,' Toby told
Emily gently. 'But to achieve that, she had to get you out
of the picture. She went mad with rage when Duarte re-
married—'

Duarte looked shaken by that information.

'I'm sorry I was such a jerk last year, Emily.' Toby
shrugged awkwardly and hovered in front of her where she
could no longer avoid looking at him. 'But to know you is
to love you and I'm a hopeless romantic. There you were,
the neglected wife—'

'She's not neglected any more,' Duarte slotted in faster
than the speed of light. 'And you told me that you fall in
love *very* easily—'

'I suppose that's true. Blame the artistic temperament.' Toby grinned at both of them, quite untouched by the smallest shade of embarrassment.

'I just wish you'd come clean with me about what Bliss was up to,' Emily censured helplessly.

'He wanted you for himself. Why would he have told you the truth about his cousin?' Duarte remarked flatly.

'I was ready to talk about Bliss after you and Duarte separated because that did make me feel bad, as it was pretty obvious that you weren't remotely interested in me. But you wouldn't talk to *me* when I trekked out to the Douro to try and sort things out,' Toby reminded Emily.

'And then I beat you up to make you stay away from her,' Duarte conceded in the thwarted undertone of someone trying to regret an action but not succeeding that well. 'You did try to get me to listen to you but I wasn't prepared to give you a hearing.'

'And after that,' Toby said with a feeling shudder, 'I was totally out of charity with you and too scared to try and talk to Emily again.'

Duarte thanked Toby for lending him his support and in doing so, ushered the younger man to the door where he urged him to enjoy his flight back to Peru.

'You're darned right I will—in your jet!' Laughing, Toby strolled out looking as if he hadn't a care in the world.

Emily watched Toby depart and felt very much like taking him by the collar and shaking him. He had caused so much trouble but it had really washed right back off him again. Easy come, easy go, that was Toby. Yet, in spite of that, Toby *had* made the effort to try and set her straight about Bliss. It was just unfortunate that she had refused to speak to him.

'I'm grateful that Jarrett was willing to provide the back-up for exposing Bliss.' Duarte shot her stilled figure a veiled glance. 'I was afraid that, without his support, you would remain suspicious.'

Emily coloured and spun away, afraid that what she was thinking would show in her face and rub salt in the wound. Duarte was so proud. Yet he had tracked down Toby and asked him for his help. She cringed inwardly at what that approach must have cost Duarte in terms of pride.

'When did you realise that Bliss was lying?' she asked uncomfortably, in one way feeling guilty that she had forced him to such lengths but in another feeling hopelessly upstaged. She had demanded proof and, no matter what the cost to himself, Duarte had supplied her with proof of Bliss's true nature. It might have taken him three weeks to track down Toby but Duarte had not called off the search. Nor had he hesitated to confess that he had been equally taken in by the other woman. Emily was extremely disconcerted by his behaviour.

'The grandfather clock...I did tell you that I had a vague recollection of Bliss once telling me about the clock—'

'No, you didn't,' she argued.

Duarte awarded her a wry smile and reminded her of how tired she had been at the end of that party three weeks earlier. 'You didn't take in what I had told you. As soon as I recalled the clock reference, I appreciated that if Bliss could lie about that, she was most probably lying about *everything*—'

'So why didn't you tell me that, the next morning?' Emily demanded.

'I still had no proof to offer that I hadn't had an affair with her,' Duarte pointed out. 'And, to be frank, I had shot myself in the foot, trying to make you jealous of her—'

'Say that again...' Emily was frowning at him, struggling to understand that sudden confession.

Duarte moved expressive and fluid hands. 'I—'

'Tell me that bit again about trying to make me jealous,'

Emily cut in a second time. 'I just want to be sure that you actually *said* that—'

Duarte was very taut. 'That conversation we had in the car after you had come to the city apartment. You had been talking about divorce again. I was angry with you. It was the impulse of a moment to exaggerate the less formal terms of my relationship with Bliss—'

'To…make…me…jealous,' Emily echoed afresh as if she was having a great deal of trouble coming to terms with that concept. 'You mean, you *lied*—'

Duarte winced at the bluntness of that term. 'At that stage, I didn't think it would do you any harm to wonder exactly what I *might* have been doing while you were staying lost in England for months on end—'

Emily folded her arms and stared at him with accusing aquamarine eyes. 'I don't believe I'm hearing this—'

'At that stage I was still suffering from the conviction that I was making a very generous gesture in trying to put our marriage back together again—'

'So you told me what was most likely to undermine it? You let me think you had got so close to Bliss—?'

'*Meu Deus*…I lived to regret my impulse, didn't I?' Duarte countered with feeling fervour. 'All I did after you went missing was work and search for you—but to confess that seemed weak!'

Emily pivoted away from him to hide a sudden helpless smile. He'd wanted to make her jealous. He had not had a clue what a nest of intrigue he was naively stirring with his behaviour. His pride had been hurting. He had been foolish but in a manner that now struck her as quite ridiculously sweet. Where was the man whom she'd once believed was so utterly indifferent to her feelings? It occurred to her that that man had never existed.

Bliss had found a fertile playground in the emotional distance between Duarte and his new wife and Emily's own shy insecurity had been the other woman's greatest aid. The blonde's first tentative efforts to cause trouble would have been swiftly concluded had Emily ever turned round and asked her husband why he never returned her phone calls.

'I have never found Bliss attractive. I was always aware of her cold nature but I did not require anything warmer from an employee whom, even now, I must concede *was* an exceptionally efficient assistant,' Duarte asserted heavily.

'When I began telling you on the flight to London about the other things she had done, you were furious with her, *not* with me...' Emily registered, turning back to look at him again, relishing that reference to Bliss as being cold.

'Of course I was furious—but more with myself even than Bliss, *minha jóia*' Duarte admitted with bleak, dark eyes of regret. 'I was bitterly angry that you had been manipulated to that extent and that I had exposed you to her malice. If I had treated you as I should have treated you, Bliss would have been powerless.'

'Yes. Just one more thing,' Emily framed with curiosity. 'The first day I came back. At the airport, you stayed with Bliss to talk to her...what about?'

'I took exception to the way in which she looked at you and spoke to you,' Duarte admitted without hesitation.

'You were telling her off.' Emily tried very hard not to laugh but for a few seconds, it was a fight she thought she would lose. She swallowed hard. She thought back to some of the things he'd said to her that same day and compared it to the speed with which he had turned on Bliss to rebuke her for what he had evidently seen as a lack of respect; she could only be amused.

'I assure you that I never ever discussed either you or our marriage with Bliss. Our more relaxed working relationship did not embrace any true confessions. I do not discuss private matters with anyone—'

'I know…' Emily conceded, fully convinced. 'Until recently, not *even* with me.'

'Right…OK, I walked right into that one,' Duarte agreed, but dark colour had risen to outline his high cheekbones.

'I just want you to appreciate that not telling me the truth about Izabel was taking confidentiality a giant step too far,' Emily murmured gently.

Duarte snatched in a sustaining breath and squared his broad shoulders. 'I believed you would think a great deal less of me if you knew what a mess my first marriage had been.'

Distressed by that patently honest admission, Emily closed the distance between them and reached for one lean brown hand. 'It wouldn't have been like that. I would have understood you much better—'

Duarte gazed down into her hugely sympathetic aquamarine eyes and murmured with brilliant golden eyes that had a rueful tinge, 'I should admit that I also rather enjoyed being treated like an omnipotent god.'

Emily blinked in disconcertion.

'It enabled me to feel in control…and I'm not in control at all!' Duarte groaned out loud with startling abruptness as he glanced at his watch and registered the time. 'We're running late for the church!'

Emily sighed. 'Look, you don't have to go through with this simply to please me. When it comes down to brass tacks, stuff like this dress and the church blessing, well…I'd much rather not have them if you really don't want them.'

'Of course I want them, *minha esposa*…' Tightening his hold on her fingers, Duarte hurried her out to the waiting limousine with quite indecent speed. 'This blessing will signify a new beginning to our marriage and a proper commitment on my part to make you happy—'

'You mean you *never* had any intention of making me happy two years ago?' Emily muttered painfully.

Duarte tucked her and her skirts into the car with careful hands and sank down beside her. 'Then the only thought in my head was making *me* happy.'

'Oh...' Only somewhat soothed by that contradiction, Emily decided that she would have to think that confession over in greater depth. 'You're saying you were totally self-ish...'

Duarte vented a reluctant laugh and closed his hand over hers again. 'I was striving to evade using exactly those words.'

The limousine drew to a halt mere minutes later outside the little village church. As Emily stepped out of the car, she was taken aback to find Victorine moving forward to present her with a beautiful bouquet of flowers and proffer stilted but evidently genuine good wishes. Emily smiled with true pleasure and thanked the older woman.

'That was so sweet of her, Duarte,' Emily enthused as her husband led her into the church, which was filled to overflowing with more flowers and lit only by candles. 'Oh, this is really lovely...'

The blessing was simple but sincere. Emily listened to every word with the happy and grateful sense that indeed she and Duarte had already found their new beginning. Her eyes damp with unashamed tears of emotion, she was startled when Duarte closed his arms round her and kissed her breathless in the shadowy darkness of the tiny church porch.

Emerging from that unexpectedly passionate clinch, Emily was flushed and in need of being guided back to the car.

'I want you to know that I have rearranged my work schedule and delegated a good deal of the business that formerly took me abroad,' Duarte informed her, studying her with intent dark golden eyes. 'This is the optimum right moment for you to make further demands, *querida*.'

Emily's mind was a terrible blank. She was in awe of this male so determined not to fall into the mistakes of the past again. Indeed, she felt just a little like a new project being enthusiastically attacked and could not help but worry about the effect of what so many sacrifices would be on him in the future. Would his first fine flush of courageous effort wear off and leave him feeling that life with her was just one big pain?

'You really don't need to *do* any more to please me. I'm not going anywhere. I'm not going to leap on the first plane back to England when we have some stupid row,' Emily assured him carefully. 'You can stop worrying.'

'I also want to admit that I totally overreacted over Toby Jarrett because, from my point of view, there was some horrible truths in what he said about my not deserving you,' Duarte ground out like a male set on an unstoppable course to tell all whether he wanted to or not. 'It was bad enough seeing him kiss you but it was worse thinking that I drove you into his arms!'

'Oh, dear...' Emily glanced at his darkly handsome profile as they walked back into the *quinta*, registering his pronounced tension with dismay.

'In fact, the weeks you were in the Douro were not exactly the best weeks of my life,' Duarte framed with charged difficulty, striding straight past the assembled household staff apparently without seeing them and carrying her with him towards the stairs. 'You see, you were still in Portugal. I had seen off Toby, dealt with him. You were still within reach...'

'Hold it a minute...' Emily urged weakly and hurried back a few steps to accept the flowers that the housekeeper was proffering and thank the older woman and their staff for the kind chorus of best wishes being offered.

Darting back to Duarte's side, breathless with her arms full of flowers, Emily prompted him helpfully, 'You were saying that while I was still within Portugal you thought of me as being still within reach...?'

Lean, powerful face rigid with tension, Duarte frowned and carried on up the stairs with Emily scurrying in his wake. 'Duarte?'

'When you vanished I was on the brink of coming to see you and asking you to come home,' Duarte completed in a charged admission.

'Please don't tell me any more...' Emily urged in a wobbly voice as tears clogged her throat. 'It's only going to make me hate myself for running away even more than I already do—'

'No. I think you had to do a vanishing act before I could admit to myself how much I loved you. And, having admitted that to myself, it sort of got it out of the way and you can be sure I didn't think about it again until very recently,' Duarte confided.

On the threshold of their bedroom, Emily surveyed him with very wide eyes of shock.

Duarte removed the flowers from her arms and settled them on the nearest piece of furniture.

'You can't leave them lying there. They'll die out of water,' Emily mumbled, no longer sure what she was saying. 'You just said that you loved me...'

Duarte closed both hands over hers and pulled her over the threshold and closed the door with a well-aimed kick.

'That is so bad for the wood,' Emily rebuked, feeling distinctly dizzy.

Duarte drew her close and splayed his fingers to her cheekbones. 'I wanted you the minute I laid eyes on you—'

'I bet you don't even *remember* the first time you laid eyes on me!' Emily objected, regarding that lesser claim as an equally contentious subject and wondering dismally in he thought that he needed to pretend that he loved her to make her happy.

A winged dark brow climbed. 'Don't I?'

'No way do you remember,' Emily told him a second time.

'You were wearing ancient jeans with holes in the knees and an old green sweater,' Duarte recounted with a certain amount of self-satisfaction. 'Your gorgeous hair was tied back with a piece of baling twine—'

'You remember...' Emily acknowledged in open disbelief at the accuracy of that description. 'But you didn't even seem to look at me—'

'So I'm subtle, *minha jóia*,' Duarte teased with glancing amusement brimming in his gaze as he absorbed her continuing shock. 'I thought you were very fanciable but I wasn't planning to do anything about it—'

Emily was hanging shamelessly on his every word. 'What changed your mind?'

'You dragged my dog out of a barn on fire and I was hugely impressed. There you were, not only sexy but nice into the bargain and so modest. Then I took you home to your family and realised you were Cinderella in disguise. All my protective instincts were roused—'

'Were they?'

Having begun, Duarte was now eager to tell all. 'I thought up that job so that I could get to know you better—'

'Without committing yourself to anything more,' Emily slotted in helplessly. 'And after you had looked your fill on me being kind and helpful with little children and animals, you asked me out to dinner with a view to what?'

'Marrying you. What's wrong with that?' Duarte went on the defensive, bright golden eyes clinging to her taut expression and troubled eyes with forceful intensity. 'OK, so I was terrified of making another mistake and I didn't rush in to asking you out—'

'It's all right. You may not have rushed in to asking me out but you did rush in to asking me to marry you,' Emily conceded but somehow still contrived to make it sound as if she had received the consolation prize.

Duarte hauled her into his arms, troubled eyes colliding with hers. 'And doesn't the fact that I couldn't wait to make you my wife tell you something?'

'You decided you'd wasted enough time observing me?'

'*Inferno!*' Duarte groaned as he stared down at her in frustration. 'I was in love with you. I just didn't want to admit that even to myself!'

She searched his lean powerful face and the intensity she met in his stunning eyes set her free forever from the belief that he did not love her. Her heart went off on a roller-coaster ride that left her breathless. 'So when did you appreciate how you felt?'

Perceptibly, Duarte winced. 'When we were separated and I started thinking that maybe I should give you a second chance—'

'It took you that long?' Emily probed unimpressed.

'Slow learner...' Possibly feeling that they had dwelt enough on his reluctance to face the strength of his feelings for her, Duarte claimed a slow deep kiss that made her pulse race.

'Just one thing you haven't explained,' Emily recalled as she surfaced. 'I assume Bliss *was* the third party who confirmed that I was supposedly having an affair with Toby—

Paling, Duarte gave her a look of deep regret. 'Who else' She said that Toby had confided in her and that she had urged him to break off the relationship—'

'That conniving little shrew—and you couldn't see the wood for the trees!' Emily condemned hotly.

'If it hadn't been for that kiss I witnessed, I wouldn'

have been so easily convinced,' Duarte argued. 'But, at the time, as far as I was concerned, Bliss had no axe to grind and every reason to avoid referring to the fact that her cousin had seduced my wife!'

'You should have had more faith in me—'

'After Izabel, trust was a problem for me. As for having more faith,' Duarte continued, deftly closing his hands to her waist and lifting her off her feet to deposit her down on the bed. He followed her down with easy grace and studied her. 'I still haven't heard an explanation of why you asked me the day I found you and Jamie if I was intending to have other women *again*?'

'Oh…that!' Her own ire doused by a dose of the same medicine, it was Emily's turn to look uncomfortable. 'Bliss never once said that you had other women but she used to sort of hint that she suspected that you strayed when you were away on business—'

'Never *once*,' Duarte delivered. 'I always valued our marriage. I would not have risked it—'

'Even when the bedroom door was locked?'

'I put that down to your being pregnant…just not being in the mood,' Duarte confided huskily. 'But when I saw you with Toby, I put a very different construction on that locked door.'

Raising a newly confident hand, Emily let her fingertips stroke down over one hard sculpted cheekbone in a loving caress. 'I love you loads and loads and loads but please don't ask me why it took me so long to decide I wanted a divorce.'

'Are you kidding?' Duarte groaned, the last of his tension dissipating as he heard those words and studied her hectically flushed face with intensely appreciative eyes of gold. 'Every time you mentioned divorce, I went into panic mode. I thought I was going to lose you again. When we were flying into London and I was facing the fact that Bliss was lying and I had got everything wrong, I felt like I was fighting for my life—'

'So that was why you were behaving that way. Sort of desperate…' Emily recalled with a heady sensation of having more power than she had ever dared to hope over the male she loved.

'And you were *so* convinced that my sole objective was hanging on to Jamie, I saw that if I told you I loved you then, there was no way on earth you were likely to believe me,' Duarte confessed with a ragged edge roughening his dark deep drawl.

'You're probably right. On the other h-hand,' Emily stammered slightly as a lean hand glided in a possessive sweep from her waist to her breast.

'You were saying, *minha jóia*?'

'I forget…' And she looked up at him, her fingers lacing into the thick black hair she loved to touch, her aquamarine eyes shimmering over him with wondering satisfaction while he slowly lowered her down on to the pillows.

Duarte frowned and abandoned her with startling abruptness. 'That reminds me.'

Emily sat up in shock and watched him stride through to his dressing room. 'Reminds you of what? Where are you going?'

Duarte emerged again with a large parcel which he balanced on the foot of the bed while he ripped off the packaging.

As Emily focused on the painting of herself which she had last seen at Toby's studio, her soft mouth opened in considerable shock.

'You were right. Toby *is* one hell of an artist. I took the painting from him because I felt that he had no right to keep an image of my wife,' Duarte informed her loftily, possessive glow in his gaze as he surveyed her. 'I intende to destroy it but, when I looked at the canvas, I could not bring myself to commit such an act of destruction.'

Emily's eyes stung. 'Now I *truly* believe that you love me—'

'Never doubt it, *minha esposa*. I will never stop loving you,' Duarte swore, abandoning the canvas to gather her back into his strong arms and claim her mouth with hot and wholly appreciative fervour.

Eighteen months later, Emily tucked Jamie into his bed Their son had learned to walk early and at supersonic speed he'd demonstrated extraordinary persistence at escaping from his cot. A little bed shaped like the toy cars he adored had seemed a safer option for their miniature mountaineer.

Smoothing his tumbled black hair from his brow, she watched him slide into the sleep of exhaustion, contentedly clutching his faded blue teddy and looking impossibly angelic. Throughout the day Jamie ran on pure livewire energy and Emily was very grateful to have not only the assistance of a nanny but also of Victorine, who had become one of Jamie's most devoted slaves. Emily adored her son too but she was already recognising many of Duarte's traits in their son. The try, try again determination, the bone-deep stubbornness and the hot temper—and she was equally grateful that Jamie had a father willing to exert loving but firm control.

There had been quite a few changes in their lives over the past eighteen months, she reflected with the lightness of heart that had become second nature to her. No longer did she worry herself sick about imminent disaster. Knowing that she was loved and valued and very much needed by Duarte had made a huge difference to her self-esteem. Even her Portuguese had improved by leaps and bounds, enabling her to overcome her former shyness and enjoy company and make proper friends.

After exchanging stilted taut phonecalls with her mother the year before in an effort to ease the tension between them and visiting again, Emily had finally acknowledged that she and her mother were never likely to be that close. Her mother's husband, Peter Davies, had never had any interest in her and that had not changed but, now that she understood why that was so, it no longer hurt her.

However, it had been a very welcome surprise when both her sisters, initially shaken by the effect of Emily finally asserting herself, had slowly come round to seeing her as she *was* rather than as the illegitimate kid sister whom they had pretty much been taught to despise. Only then had she realised how easily families could all sink into the same bad pattern of behaviour. She had finally appreciated that neither Hermione nor Corinne were that close to Lorene either but over the past year her sisters had steadily become closer to Emily.

'They just copied your mother. It wasn't until you made them stand back and question their attitude that they saw how it had been. They're adults now and they've started thinking for themselves,' Duarte had asserted with immense approval, no longer referring to them as the ugly sisters and indeed making much-appreciated efforts to introduce them to eligible men.

And Duarte? Emily crossed the corridor into their bedroom—the nursery had been moved to a more convenien location. Emily smiled as she noticed the adrenalin kit i the bedroom—Duarte had insisted they had one in ever room.

Duarte strolled out of the bathroom, still wet from th shower, only a towel wrapped round his lean hips. 'Is Jami asleep?'

He still took her breath away, Emily conceded, strivin not to stare like a teenager at all that potent masculinity o display. 'Out like a light—'

'It'll be the five o'clock start he had today.' Duarte gave a slight shudder at the memory of being bounced into rude wakefulness at dawn by his energetic son.

'Oh, well,' Emily said wickedly. 'You are the man who once wanted a really big family and I have reached a decision—'

Duarte had tensed. 'What about?'

'I want another baby—'

'Two to bounce on us at dawn?' Duarte tried to tease but shock was written all over him at that announcement. 'Emily, you really *don't* have to make the kind of sacrifice for me. There's a lot more to family than numbers. I'm perfectly happy with Jamie—'

'But I'm not and this has very little to do with you,' Emily told him with dancing eyes, touched by his efforts to dissuade her when she knew how much he regretted never having had the opportunity to really share her last pregnancy with her. 'I just have this yen for another child—'

Duarte searched her smiling face with a frown and he argued, 'I don't want you being sick and miserable—'

'But it's not going to be like that again—'

'How do you know?'

'I *know*,' Emily told him with an air of feminine superiority. 'I just know…OK?'

He reached for her and drew her lazily up against his big powerful body, sending her temperature rocketing. Stunning golden eyes glittered over her with possessive heat. 'It's just we come first and I want you to be happy—'

'You're the man who promised me the moon,' Emily said plaintively, lashes cast down. 'I'm *still* waiting…'

Duarte vented a deeply appreciative laugh and backed her down on the bed. 'Are you ever going to let me live that down, *minha esposa*?'

'Probably not.' She smiled up at him, her heart in her eyes, luxuriating in the adoring look he could not hide, thinking how lucky she was and how gloriously happy. It had not taken the gift of the moon to bring about that transformation. All it had taken was love.

'I love you more every day,' Duarte groaned hungrily against her extended throat, feeling her quiver and arch in instant encouragement. 'You've got me flying home for lunch now. You make me insatiable—'

'Hear any complaints?' Emily teased, inching off his towel like a shameless woman set on seduction. 'Instead of some boring working lunch, you get me—'

'And the more I get of you, the more I want you,' Duarte confided, stringing a trail of tormenting kisses across her delicate collarbone. 'OK…we'll think about another baby when we've really talked over the idea in depth.'

Arabel Monteiro was born nine months and two weeks later and their daughter's conception never was discussed in depth. Emily was neither sick nor miserable during her second pregnancy and Duarte presented her with a very beautiful diamond-studded moonstone pendant and earrings.

'You're not getting off the hook that easily,' Emily warned him cheerfully.

'I think you finally know me, *minha esposa*,' Duarte pronounced with loving eyes and his wonderful smile.

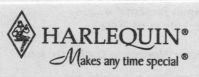

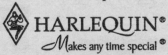

Harlequin truly does make any time special. . . . This year we are celebrating weddings in style!

A Walk Down the Aisle
WEDDING CELEBRATION

To help us celebrate, we want you to tell us how wearing the Harlequin wedding gown will make your wedding day special. As the grand prize, Harlequin will offer one lucky bride the chance to **"Walk Down the Aisle"** in the Harlequin wedding gown!

There's more...

For her honeymoon, she and her groom will spend five nights at the **Hyatt Regency Maui.** As part of this five-night honeymoon at the hotel renowned for its romantic attractions, the couple will enjoy a candlelit dinner for two in Swan Court, a sunset sail on the hotel's catamaran, and duet spa treatments.

A HYATT RESORT AND SPA

Maui • Molokai • Lanai

To enter, please write, in, 250 words or less, how wearing the Harlequin wedding gown will make your wedding day special. The entry will be judged based on its emotionally compelling nature, its originality and creativity, and its sincerity. This contest is open to Canadian and U.S. residents only and to those who are 18 years of age and older. There is no purchase necessary to enter. Void where prohibited. See further contest rules attached. Please send your entry to:

Walk Down the Aisle Contest

In Canada	In U.S.A.
P.O. Box 637	P.O. Box 9076
Fort Erie, Ontario	3010 Walden Ave.
L2A 5X3	Buffalo, NY 14269-9076

You can also enter by visiting www.eHarlequin.com
Win the Harlequin wedding gown and the vacation of a lifetime!
The deadline for entries is October 1, 2001.

HARLEQUIN®
Makes any time special ®

HARLEQUIN WALK DOWN THE AISLE TO MAUI CONTEST 1197
OFFICIAL RULES
NO PURCHASE NECESSARY TO ENTER

1. To enter, follow directions published in the offer to which you are responding. Contest begins April 2, 2001, and ends on October 1, 2001. Method of entry may vary. Mailed entries must be postmarked by October 1, 2001, and received by October 8, 2001.

2. Contest entry may be, at times, presented via the Internet, but will be restricted solely to residents of certain geographic areas that are disclosed on the Web site. To enter via the Internet, if permissible, access the Harlequin Web site (www.eHarlequin.com) and follow the directions displayed online. Online entries must be received by 11:59 p.m. E.S.T. on October 1, 2001.

   In lieu of submitting an entry online, enter by mail by hand-printing (or typing) on an 8½" x 11" plain piece of paper, your name, address (including zip code), Contest number/name and in 250 words or fewer, why winning a Harlequin wedding dress would make your wedding day special. Mail via first-class mail to: Harlequin Walk Down the Aisle Contest 1197, (in the U.S.) P.O. Box 9076, 3010 Walden Avenue, Buffalo, NY 14269-9076, (in Canada) P.O. Box 637, Fort Erie, Ontario L2A 5X3, Canada.

   Limit one entry per person, household address and e-mail address. Online and/or mailed entries received from persons residing in geographic areas in which Internet entry is not permissible will be disqualified.

3. Contests will be judged by a panel of members of the Harlequin editorial, marketing and public relations staff based on the following criteria:
   - Originality and Creativity—50%
   - Emotionally Compelling—25%
   - Sincerity—25%

   In the event of a tie, duplicate prizes will be awarded. Decisions of the judges are final.

4. All entries become the property of Torstar Corp. and will not be returned. No responsibility is assumed for lost, late, illegible, incomplete, inaccurate, nondelivered or misdirected mail or misdirected e-mail, for technical, hardware or software failures of any kind, lost or unavailable network connections, or failed, incomplete, garbled or delayed computer transmission or any human error which may occur in the receipt or processing of the entries in this Contest.

5. Contest open only to residents of the U.S. (except Puerto Rico) and Canada, who are 18 years of age or older, and is void wherever prohibited by law; all applicable laws and regulations apply. Any litigation within the Province of Quebec respecting the conduct or organization of a publicity contest may be submitted to the Régie des alcools, des courses et des jeux for a ruling. Any litigation respecting the awarding of a prize may be submitted to the Régie des alcools, des courses et des jeux only for the purpose of helping the parties reach a settlement. Employees and immediate family members of Torstar Corp. and D. L. Blair, Inc., their affiliates, subsidiaries and all other agencies, entities and persons connected with the use, marketing or conduct of this Contest are not eligible to enter. Taxes on prizes are the sole responsibility of winners. Acceptance of any prize offered constitutes permission to use winner's name, photograph or other likeness for the purposes of advertising, trade and promotion on behalf of Torstar Corp., its affiliates and subsidiaries without further compensation to the winner, unless prohibited by law.

6. Winners will be determined no later than November 15, 2001, and will be notified by mail. Winners will be required to sign and return an Affidavit of Eligibility form within 15 days after winner notification. Noncompliance within that time period may result in disqualification and an alternative winner may be selected. Winner of trip must execute a Release of Liability prior to ticketing and must possess required travel documents (e.g. passport, photo ID) where applicable. Trip must be completed by November 2002. No substitution of prize permitted by winner. Torstar Corp. and D. L. Blair, Inc., their parents, affiliates, and subsidiaries are not responsible for errors in printing or electronic presentation of Contest, entries and/or game pieces. In the event of printing or other errors which may result in unintended prize values or duplication of prizes, all affected game pieces or entries shall be null and void. If for any reason the Internet portion of the Contest is not capable of running as planned, including infection by computer virus, bugs, tampering, unauthorized intervention, fraud, technical failures, or any other causes beyond the control of Torstar Corp. which corrupt or affect the administration, secrecy, fairness, integrity or proper conduct of the Contest, Torstar Corp. reserves the right, at its sole discretion, to disqualify any individual who tampers with the entry process and to cancel, terminate, modify or suspend the Contest or the Internet portion thereof. In the event of a dispute regarding an online entry, the entry will be deemed submitted by the authorized holder of the e-mail account submitted at the time of entry. Authorized account holder is defined as the natural person who is assigned to an e-mail address by an Internet access provider, online service provider or other organization that is responsible for arranging e-mail address for the domain associated with the submitted e-mail address. **Purchase or acceptance of a product offer does not improve your chances of winning.**

   Prizes: (1) Grand Prize—A Harlequin wedding dress (approximate retail value: $3,500) and a 5-night/6-day honeymoon trip to Maui, HI, including round-trip air transportation provided by Maui Visitors Bureau from Los Angeles International Airport (winner is responsible for transportation to and from Los Angeles International Airport) and a Harlequin Romance Package, including hotel accomodations (double occupancy) at the Hyatt Regency Maui Resort and Spa, dinner for (2) two at Swan Court, a sunset sail on Kiele V and a spa treatment for the winner (approximate retail value: $4,000); (5) Five runner-up prizes of a $1000 gift certificate to selected retail outlets to be determined by Sponsor (retail value $1000 ea.). Prizes consist of only those items listed as part of the prize. Limit one prize per person. All prizes are valued in U.S. currency.

   For a list of winners (available after December 17, 2001) send a self-addressed, stamped envelope to: Harlequin Walk Down the Aisle Contest 1197 Winners, P.O. Box 4200 Blair, NE 68009-4200 or you may access the www.eHarlequin.com Web site through January 15, 2002.

Contest sponsored by Torstar Corp., P.O. Box 9042, Buffalo, NY 14269-9042, U.S.A.

PHWDACONT2